"You're my boss. I'm your secretary."

There was triumph in Lucas's silver eyes as he replied, "You want me, Kim. Your lips and body told me that this morning."

"*Lucas.*" Kim glanced around nervously.

"And sooner or later it will happen," he continued silkily. "You know that as well as I do. That's why you've been so jumpy from the first day you came to work for me...."

HELEN BROOKS lives in Northamptonshire, England, and is married with three children. As she is a committed Christian, busy housewife and mother, her spare time is at a premium, but her hobbies include reading, swimming, gardening and walking her two energetic, inquisitive and very endearing young dogs. Her long-cherished aspiration to write became a reality when she put pen to paper on reaching the age of forty, and sent the result off to Harlequin Mills & Boon.

Books by Helen Brooks

HARLEQUIN PRESENTS®
2237—A WHIRLWIND MARRIAGE
2255—THE GREEK TYCOON'S BRIDE

Helen Brooks

THE IRRESISTIBLE TYCOON

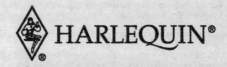

TORONTO • NEW YORK • LONDON
AMSTERDAM • PARIS • SYDNEY • HAMBURG
STOCKHOLM • ATHENS • TOKYO • MILAN • MADRID
PRAGUE • WARSAW • BUDAPEST • AUCKLAND

ISBN 0-373-12281-0

THE IRRESISTIBLE TYCOON

First North American Publication 2002.

Copyright © 2001 by Helen Brooks.

CHAPTER ONE

'KIM, I'm not at all sure that this is the right step to take, I'm really not. You've enough on your plate as it is; you know that.'

'I've no choice, Maggie, and *you* know *that*,' Kim answered steadily.

'But...' Maggie Conway stared helplessly at her friend as she ran out of words.

'Look, just be an angel and pick up Melody after school, okay? I shouldn't be much later than five but you know how interviews are; they might keep me waiting for a while.'

'No problem,' Maggie said unhappily.

'Thanks. I don't know what I'd do without you,' Kim said with heartfelt warmth as she gave Maggie a brief hug.

Kim was still thinking about her last words as she left the comfort of Maggie's spacious, open-plan apartment and stepped into the crisp frosty air outside the big Victorian house which had been converted into several self-contained flats.

Maggie was an unlikely-looking angel, being as round as she was tall with a shock of vibrant curly ginger hair and freckles covering every inch of her skin, but an angel she was nevertheless, Kim told herself silently as she walked briskly to the bus stop. How she would have got through the last two traumatic years without Maggie's unfailing support and good humour she didn't know.

She reached the bus stop just as the bus drew round the corner and, once seated, stared unseeingly out of the window, quite oblivious to the overt stare of the young, good-looking man sitting opposite her who clearly couldn't take his eyes off the golden-haired beauty on the other side of the aisle.

Maggie had stepped in as unpaid childminder when the need arose—as it did frequently—confidante, stalwart friend, advisor and a whole host of other roles, Kim reflected warmly. The only good thing to come out of her relationship with Graham—apart from Melody, of course—was that he had introduced her to Maggie.

Graham... Kim's soft full mouth tightened and her brown eyes narrowed for a moment before she forced her thoughts away from the spectre in her mind.

This wasn't the time to think of Graham, not with such an important interview looming, she told herself firmly, straightening in the seat and squaring her slender shoulders. She understood the competition for the post of secretary to the chairman and managing director of Kane Electrical was fierce, and she needed to be focused and clear from the outset.

It was another fifteen minutes before the bus dropped her on the outskirts of Cambridge and almost outside the huge site which Kane Electrical occupied, and within five minutes she was standing in Reception explaining to the model-slim, beautifully coiffured receptionist that she had an appointment with Mr Lucas Kane at half-past two.

'Right.' The girl's expertly made-up eyes had made a swift summing up of the tall, discreetly dressed woman in front of her, and now she gave a practised smile as she said blandly, 'If you would like to take a seat for a moment I'll tell Mr Kane's secretary you're here, Mrs Allen.'

'Thank you.' Kim had flushed slightly under the scrutiny. Her winter coat was a good one, but not new, neither were her shoes and handbag, whereas the receptionist's expertly cut grey silk suit screamed a designer label and her hair could only have been cut by one of the most expensive salons in Cambridge.

Still, she wasn't going to let this girl or anyone else intimidate her, Kim told herself fiercely as she took the proffered seat and sank into inches of soft leather upholstery. She might not be wearing the very latest fashion or have her hair styled by Vidal Sassoon but she was an excellent secretary, as her references confirmed.

She raised her small chin abruptly and stared straight ahead, her hands resting in her lap and her knees demurely together, before a restrained commotion at the side of her— as a tall, dark man with what could only be described as an entourage swept into the building—brought her head swinging round.

Whether it was the receptionist's less than tactful appraisal, or the fact that everyone on the perimeter of the man seemed to be falling over themselves to get his attention, Kim didn't know, but she found herself staring at the back of the personage in question with unmitigated dislike.

He certainly knew how to make an entrance, she thought waspishly, and he was so full of his own importance he was almost bursting with it! How she disliked the fawning and obsequious servility that went with wealth and power in some quarters.

The party was making for the lifts at the far side of the reception in a subdued furore of which the man leading seemed totally unaware, and Kim still had her eyes fixed on his back, her face expressing her feelings only too clearly, when he suddenly turned and to her shock and surprise looked straight at her.

She was conscious of a pair of rivetingly hard, metallic silver-grey eyes taking in the whole of her in a stunningly swift perusal that was quite devastating before she could wipe her face of all expression, and then she saw dark

eyebrows rise in mordant disdain. The message was unmistakable.

He had recognised what she was thinking, recognised it
and dismissed it—and her—as beneath his contempt, she
thought as her face turned scarlet. And she couldn't blame
him, she really couldn't. If nothing else she had been un-
forgivably rude.

In the split second before the lift doors opened and the
man turned to enter Kim's mind raced, but there was no
time to do anything but watch him disappear. The doors
closed, there was the faintest of purrs as the lift ascended,
and that was that.

She was aware of sinking back in the seat and it was
only then she became conscious she had been holding herself rigid. How embarrassing! She shut her eyes for the
briefest of moments and swallowed hard, glancing across
at the receptionist, who was speaking to someone on the
telephone. What must he have thought? But then he'd left
her in no doubt what he had thought, she added with a
touch of dark humour.

She was looking at the receptionist without seeing her
now, her mind continuing to dissect every moment of the
little drama which had unfurled so unexpectedly. Who was
he? Obviously someone important: one of the directors of
the firm maybe?

An awful thought occurred to her but she pushed it away
immediately. No, it wouldn't be him—not Lucas Kane, she
told herself firmly. That would be too disastrous, and if
nothing else she was due some good fortune—well over-
due, as it happened.

'Mrs Allen?'

Kim came out of her rueful musing with a little jolt to
find a tall, rather formidable-looking woman standing in
front of her.

'Good afternoon.' A hand was extended and as Kim rose

she made a suitable reply, shaking the other woman's hand. 'I'm June West,' the woman continued, 'Mr Kane's secretary. If you would like to come with me...'

'Thank you.' As they walked towards the waiting lift Kim glanced at the other woman from under her eyelashes. June West was the person the successful applicant would have to follow, and if Lucas Kane's present secretary was anything like as efficient as she looked they would have their work cut out. It didn't help Kim's confidence an iota.

'Mr Kane is running a little late.' As the lift doors closed, June turned to her with a polite smile. 'We've had one panic after another this morning.'

Kim nodded, smiling in turn before she said, 'Is that usual? The panics, I mean?'

'I'm afraid so.' June was looking hard at her. 'As his secretary you would have to be used to working under pressure most of the time and making decisions for yourself. Would that be a problem?'

Being under pressure and making decisions for herself? That had been her life for the last two years—and before— Kim reflected silently. 'No. No, it wouldn't.'

'Good.' The smile was warmer now. 'I've worked for Mr Kane for the last ten years and I can honestly say there's never been a dull moment. It hasn't always been easy, and the job is certainly not your average nine-to-five, but he's a very fair employer and prepared to give and take, if you know what I mean.'

Kim didn't, not really, but she nodded and said, 'Can I ask why you are leaving?'

'Of course. Sensible question.' The lift doors had opened and now Kim followed the tall figure into a hushed corridor as June said over her shoulder, 'I'm getting married and my future husband lives and works in Scotland. He's got his own business; I met him through Kane Electrical, actually, as he's one of our suppliers, so it's not feasible for him to make the move.'

'Congratulations,' Kim said with genuine cordiality.

'Thanks.' As June opened a door and waved Kim through, she added quietly, 'I'd given up on meeting the man of my dreams, to be honest, but whoever said life begins at forty was dead right as far as I was concerned.'

So June was forty, and she had obviously been a career woman dedicated to her job and Kane Electrical for the last decade—she had been right about the other woman being a hard act to follow if nothing else, Kim thought ruefully.

'This is my office.'

They were standing in a large, beautifully decorated room with ankle-deep carpet and the very latest in office furniture and equipment, Kim noted.

'And through there—' June inclined her head to a door behind her desk '—is my private cloakroom. Mr Kane has his own leading off his office along with a dressing room and small sitting room. He sometimes sleeps over when things are particularly hectic,' she added quietly.

'Right.' This was way, way out of her league. Kim kept her face expressionless but her thoughts were racing. The best she could hope for was to get through the next twenty minutes—or however long the interview with Lucas Kane lasted—without making a complete fool of herself. He was clearly looking for a personal assistant-cum-secretary who would eat, breathe and sleep Kane Electrical, and she just couldn't give that degree of commitment with Melody to consider.

But she had stated quite clearly she had a four-year-old daughter on her CV, she reminded herself in the next instant, divesting herself of her coat before taking the seat June indicated and watching the other woman disappear through the interconnecting door in to her boss's domain.

She wouldn't have got this far if he objected to his secretary having a life outside of work, would she?

She glanced round the opulent room again and her stomach swirled. She was amazed she *had* got this far if she was being honest, she admitted silently. It had been the thought of the huge salary such a post would command— nothing more and nothing less—which had prompted her to send off her CV when she had seen the position advertised at the end of September, just over four weeks ago now.

She hadn't heard anything at all for three weeks and then she had received a letter, written on embossed, thick linen notepaper, stating she had been selected for the initial short list to attend an interview on Monday, 30th October, at 2.30 p.m.

Which was today, now, this very minute! *Oh, help.*

'Mrs Allen?' June had opened the interconnecting door again and was smiling at her. 'Mr Kane will see you now.'

She knew, just a moment before she walked through the door, who would be seated within the room beyond. It was in that split second Kim acknowledged she had had a presentiment the moment she had stared into the cold silver eyes in the lobby below. He had *looked* like a millionaire tycoon; it had been in his walk, his bearing, the turn of his head, even the way his eyes had held hers in such arrogant contempt and disregard.

'Mrs Allen...' A tall, broad-shouldered figure rose from behind a massive grey desk at her approach, but the clear autumn sunlight streaming in through the huge plate-glass window behind him blinded Kim for a moment and turned Lucas Kane into a dark silhouette. And then, as she reached the chair which had been placed in front of the desk, she blinked, and he came into focus. Alarmingly into focus. All six feet four, and then some, of him!

'How do you do?' He was smiling as he enclosed her

small paw in his long fingers, but it was definitely a croc-
odile sort of smile, Kim noted helplessly. He had obviously
realised who she was earlier and had been looking forward
to this moment with some relish. 'Please be seated, Mrs
Allen.'

She wasn't going to give him the satisfaction of stutter-
ing and stammering, and she knew she wouldn't be able to
speak clearly until she had had a moment or two to pull
herself together, so she smiled in what she hoped was a
cool, contained sort of way and sank gracefully into the
chair. If nothing else it eased her trembling legs!

There hadn't been time to look beyond the granite stare
which had pinned her down in Reception, but now, to add
to the agitation and shock that had her heart thumping like
a sledgehammer, she could see Lucas Kane was disturbingly attractive. Not handsome, the rugged chiselled face
and impressive muscled body was too aggressively male
and ruthlessly compelling to ever be labelled such, but he
had something that went far beyond good looks.

'You understand you are one of four applicants on a final
short list?' he asked expressionlessly without looking at
her, his eyes on the papers on his desk as his hand flicked
over a page of what she assumed was her CV.

His hair was very black, almost a blue-black, she noted
silently, and cut so short as to be harshly severe. And then
he raised his head, and the curiously silver eyes shaded by
thick black lashes compelled a response.

'Yes, I do, Mr Kane,' she managed evenly.

'So what makes you think I should choose you over the
other excellent candidates?' he drawled smoothly, but with
an edge that told her the incident in Reception was not
forgotten or forgiven.

She had had the answer to just such a question drilled
into her during the business management degree she had
taken at university, and had even encountered it first-hand

when she had applied for her last job, just over two years ago, but now, in the face of Lucas Kane's cruelly mocking scrutiny, something hot and contumacious rose up in Kim's chest.

'That's for you to weigh in the balance and consider, surely, Mr Kane,' she answered coolly.

The silver eyes iced over a fraction more; her tone of voice clearly hadn't been to his liking. 'Is it, indeed?' It was soft and low but with an underlying sharpness that suggested velvet disguising pure steel.

He had expected a stock answer—she had read that in the brief dart of surprise the silver-grey eyes had been unable to conceal—but she wasn't playing any sort of game with this man. If he wanted to conduct a straightforward interview that was one thing, but she wasn't going to be intimidated by Lucas Kane or anyone else.

He stared at her for another moment or two and she forced herself not to drop her gaze, and then he flicked the intercom on his desk.

'Yes, Mr Kane?' June's voice sounded so wonderfully normal it made Kim want to get up and fly into the outer office.

'Coffee, June, for Mrs Allen and myself.'

Kim had been half expecting him to tell his secretary that the interview was finished, or ask June to show her out—anything, in fact, but request coffee for them both. She found she badly wanted to smooth her hair but restrained the impulse to fiddle with the thick shining braid coiled tightly on top of her head, knowing the intuitive, razor-sharp mind on the other side of the desk would recognise the nervousness behind such a gesture.

'Or perhaps you would prefer tea?' The brilliant gaze had fastened on her again after the brief respite.

'Coffee will be fine, thank you,' she answered carefully, keeping her voice in neutral.

'So, Mrs Allen...'

His voice was very distinctive, she thought shakily as she watched him settle himself comfortably in the vast leather chair and lean back slightly, crossing one long leg over the other knee as he surveyed her unblinkingly. Deep and ever so slightly husky, with the merest trace of an accent she couldn't quite place.

'Are you a career woman?' he asked softly.

There was only one answer she could possibly give to such a leading question, given the circumstances; a reply in the affirmative was what he was expecting and what she must make—the knowledge was screamingly obvious. 'My work is very important to me, Mr Kane, yes,' Kim said quickly. But not necessarily for the reasons he supposed, she added silently.

'And I see you got a First at university. That must mean you worked hard but had a natural aptitude for the subject too?' he commented thoughtfully.

She couldn't read anything from either his tone or his face but somehow she felt a punchline was on the way, and she couldn't quite keep the wariness out of her voice when she said, 'Yes, I suppose so.'

She saw the firm hard mouth twitch slightly, as though he was enjoying some private joke of his own, but his voice was still very even—almost expressionless—as he continued, 'So why did you get married immediately on graduating from university, and moreover start a family within months, if you intended to make the most of your excellent qualifications and carve a career for yourself? It doesn't quite seem to add up, Mrs Allen.'

Flipping cheek! She thought about making some facetious reply and passing off what she considered an extremely intrusive question, but he had hit her on the raw—possibly because she had had cause to bitterly regret the marriage almost immediately—so her voice was cold when she replied, 'Whether it adds up or not, that is what happened, Mr Kane, and it is my business, no one else's.' Okay, so she'd blown it good and proper, she thought sickly, but she didn't want his rotten job anyway!

She expected a cutting retort, something stinging to put her in her place, but even as she had started speaking he had straightened in his seat and was bending over the papers again, his voice businesslike as he said, 'Did you meet your husband at university?'

'Yes.' It was succinct in the extreme but he didn't look up.

'And I see you were widowed barely three years later. That must have been hard for you.'

There was nothing she could say to that and so she kept quiet, but he obviously didn't expect a comment as he continued immediately, 'That would have meant your daughter was two years of age when you became a single-parent family?'

'Yes.'

'Tough break.'

There was a smokier quality to his voice as he spoke, a trace of warmth evident in the deep husky tones for the first time, and it unnerved her. Kim didn't know why it bothered her but it did, and she suddenly found she was acutely aware of the formidable breadth of his shoulders and the muscled strength evident beneath the superficial veneer of expensive cloth.

It took all coherent thought clean away, and in the pause which followed Lucas Kane raised his dark head, his piercing eyes narrowing on her troubled face. 'You find it painful to talk about this, Mrs Allen?' he asked quietly.

Kim nodded—it seemed the safest option—but she was heartily thankful he had misunderstood the reason for her evident agitation.

'I think you can appreciate I have to ask whether you

have suitable arrangements in place should the need arise for you to work late or even be away from home for a few days?' he continued expressionlessly after another brief pause. 'Such occurrences are not unusual in this office.'

'Yes, I do.' This was more solid ground and Kim's large chocolate-brown eyes expressed the sentiment to the perceptive metallic gaze watching her so closely, although she was unaware of it.

'Melody was in full-time nursery care for two years before she started school in September and she loved it,' Kim said quickly, 'and she's just sailed into school. The school provides an after-hours club for children with working parents which finishes at five-thirty, but if ever I'm unavailable to pick her up a good friend who lives close by and works from home steps in. If I had to go on a business trip, Maggie would love to have her for however long it took.'

'How fortuitous.'

It was even and spoken without any expression but somehow Kim felt an implied criticism in the smooth tone. Her eyes narrowed and she stared hard into the tough masculine face in front of her, but other than ask him outright if he had a problem with the way she organised her affairs she could do nothing but say, coolly, 'Yes, it is. I'm very fortunate to have a friend like Maggie.'

'You don't have family living near?'

'No. My...my husband was an only child and his parents had him late in life. They're now in their sixties and his father is in poor health so they rarely travel from Scotland, where they live.'

'And your family?' he persisted relentlessly.

What this had to do with her aptitude to do the job, she didn't know! 'I have no family,' she said shortly.

'*None?*'

He sounded faintly incredulous and she supposed she couldn't blame him. 'I was orphaned as a young child,' she said matter-of-factly. 'I lived with an elderly aunt for a time but when she died and left her estate to her own family I was put in a children's home.'

The silver-grey eyes flickered briefly.

'So,' Kim continued quietly, 'I suppose I might have some distant relatives somewhere but I wouldn't go so far as to call them family, and I certainly have no wish to trace any of them. I've made my own life and that's the way I like it.'

He leant back in the chair again, his eyes never leaving her face. 'I see.'

Exactly what he saw Kim wasn't sure, but she felt she had as much chance of being offered this job as a snowball in hell.

'Since your husband died you have worked for Mr Curtis of Curtis & Brackley, is that right? And the firm went into liquidation four weeks ago.' He was reading from her CV again and the relief of having that laser-sharp gaze off her face was overwhelming.

'Which is when I saw this job advertised,' Kim agreed.

'Mr Curtis seems to have thought a great deal of you. He has written what I can only describe as a glowing reference.'

And she had earned it. Hours of overtime a week; calls in to the office to deal with minor panics at weekends; interrupted holidays—Bob Curtis had had no compunction in wringing every last working minute he could out of her. But the salary had been good and Curtis & Brackley had been practically on her doorstep and just down the street from Melody's nursery. But it had been the memory of trailing from interview to interview, in the span between Graham's death and securing a job, that had induced her to put up with almost anything.

Bob had been kind enough in his own way and she had found the running of the small office exerted no great pressure or stress; indeed in the last six months she had been becoming increasingly bored.

'It was a nice family firm to work for,' Kim said now as she realised Lucas Kane was waiting for a response.

'Kane Electrical is not a nice family firm,' came the dry reply as the eagle eyes flashed to meet hers again. 'Do you think you are capable of making the transition?'

It wasn't so much what he said but the way in which he said it, and again it caught Kim on the raw, calling forth a terse reply that was not like her, she thought confusedly even as she said, 'I wouldn't have wasted your time or mine in applying for the position if I didn't, Mr Kane.'

She saw the dark brows frown and his mouth tighten, but June chose that precise moment to knock and enter with the coffee, and Kim had never been so pleased to see anyone in her life. She knew she was flushed, she could feel her cheeks burning, and she acknowledged her tone had not been one which a prospective employee would dream of using to their future employer, but it was *him*, Lucas Kane, she told herself in silent agitation. She had never met such a patronising, arrogant, downright *supercilious* man in all her life.

'Do you own a car, Mrs Allen?'

'What?' She had just settled back in her seat after accepting her cup of coffee from June and was bringing the cup to her lips when the question, barked as it was, made the steaming hot coffee slurp over the side of the china cup into the saucer as Kim gave an involuntary start.

'A car?' he repeated very distinctly.

The tone was now one of exaggerated patience, and it brought the adrenalin pumping again as she took a deep breath and forced herself not to bite back, instead speaking calmly and coolly as she said, 'No, I do not own a car, Mr Kane.'

'But I see you have passed a driving test. Are you a

confident driver?' His eyes were like narrowed points of silver light. 'Or perhaps I should ask if you are a competent one?' he added silkily.

'I'm both confident and competent,' she answered smartly. 'Maggie has me on her insurance so I borrow her car when I need to.'

'Ah, the ever-helpful Maggie.'

She *definitely* didn't like his tone, and she had just opened her mouth to tell him so, and to point out what he could do with his wonderful job, when he said, 'If you were offered this post and accepted it a car would be provided for your use. A BMW or something similar. I don't want my secretary trailing about waiting for buses that arrive late, or being unable to get from A to B in the shortest possible time.'

She stared at him, uncertain of what to say. Was he telling her all this so that she would be aware of what she had missed when he turned her down? she asked herself wretchedly. She wouldn't put anything past Lucas Kane.

'And there would be a clothing allowance,' he continued smoothly, his gaze running over her for a second and reminding her that her off-the-peg suit—although smart and businesslike—was not in the same league as the couturier number June was wearing. 'There is the occasional function here in England which requires evening dress, but certainly on the trips abroad you will require an array of clothes.'

If she had been flushed before she knew she was like a beetroot now. He had put it fairly tactfully, she had to admit, but the end result was that he considered her an office version of Cinderella! But clothing for herself *had* been the last priority since Graham had died, in fact she couldn't remember buying anything new since then, apart from items of underwear. She just hadn't been able to afford it...

'Yes, I see.' She forced the words out through stiff lips

and then took a hefty sip of the hot coffee, letting it burn a fortifying path down into her stomach.

He didn't have a clue how the other half lived, she thought savagely, shading her eyes with her thick lashes so he wouldn't see the anger in her eyes. For the last two years she had lain awake nearly every night doing interminable sums in her head, even though she knew the end result would be fruitless.

Her marriage had been a nightmare but Graham's death—following a drinking binge when he had fallen through a shop plate-glass window—had unleashed a whole new set of horrors. Her husband had left debts—frightening, mind-boggling debts, as far as she was concerned—and, Graham being Graham, he hadn't been concerned about tying her into the terrifying tangle. She had been so *stupid* in the early days of their marriage; she'd trusted him, signed papers without enquiring too much about the whys and wherefores, and the payments she'd believed had been as regular as clockwork just hadn't happened.

Not only that but he had borrowed from friends, business colleagues, *anyone* who would lend him money to finance his failing one-man business and—more importantly, to Graham—his alcohol addiction.

She had known, once she had become pregnant with Melody, there was something terribly wrong. The handsome, charming, flashing-eyed Romeo from university days had changed into someone she didn't recognise, but she had put it down to work stress, the unplanned pregnancy—she had become pregnant following a stomach bug which had made the Pill ineffective—all manner of things but the real cause.

She had loved him, made excuses for him—fool, fool, *fool*. And all the while the debts had been mounting, debts she was now struggling to pay off, month after painful month, as well as providing for her daughter and herself.

Maggie had been great. The two thousand pounds Graham had borrowed from her had been written off as far as Maggie was concerned on the day of the funeral, but there were plenty of others who hadn't been so magnanimous.

She was constantly torn all ways. She wanted Melody to have nice clothes, good food and a happy environment, but although she had struggled to make the best of the tiny bedsit she had rented since the funeral it was hardly the best place in the world in which to bring up a young child. And the debts diminished so slowly. She couldn't believe how slowly.

'I take it you could start immediately, Mrs Allen, should you be offered the post?'

Kim had been so entrenched in the morass of the past that her eyes were almost bewildered when she raised them to meet Lucas Kane's.

'Yes, I… Yes.' Pull yourself together and act like the efficient secretary he's looking for, she told herself bitterly. You can't afford to be choosy about who you work for, even though you disliked this man on sight. Not that she had any chance of securing the post; he had made that very clear.

'And would you accept the position, should it be offered?' he asked softly.

She stared at him, her stomach muscles tightening as she acknowledged again that she felt he was playing with her. And she had had enough of that—manipulation, half-truths, deceit—to last her a lifetime.

'Oh, I'm sorry, I should have mentioned the salary before now.' His voice was very cool as he mentioned a figure that was three times as much as she had been getting at Curtis & Brackley.

Kim gaped at him. She knew her mouth was partly open,

that was the worst of it, but she was too stunned to do anything about it.

'I believe in paying the best for the best, Mrs Allen.' His mouth was twisted in a quizzical smile. 'But if you worked for me you would earn every penny; ask Miss West if you don't believe me. I demand absolute loyalty, unquestioning allegiance to Kane Electrical... You get my drift?'

His derisive expression was mocking but in this instant Kim found she didn't care. Her mind was turning cartwheels in working out what such a financial bonus would mean and, on top of a car, a dress allowance... But she hadn't been offered the job. She came back to earth with a wallop.

'I...I think with such a generous package you would be within your rights to expect complete commitment and dedication from your secretary, Mr Kane,' she managed at last. And how!

'You do? Good. A meeting point at last.' His voice was very deep and quiet and for a moment the portent of his words didn't register. And then, as the covert censure hit, Kim flushed hotly.

The silver gaze ran over her pink face, the golden-blonde of her upswept hair bringing the charcoal-brown of her eyes into greater contrast, and then Lucas Kane stood up abruptly, thrusting his hands into his pockets as he turned to look out of the huge window behind him.

'You haven't answered my question, Mrs Allen.' His voice was remote, distant.

'I haven't?' Her mind was whirling and for a second she couldn't grasp what he was getting at.

'I asked you if you would accept the position if it was offered,' he reminded her evenly, still without turning round.

She stared at the big figure in front of her, part of her mind conceding that he must be one of the tallest men she had ever met and certainly the most disturbing, and then she found herself saying, 'Yes, I would accept it, Mr Kane, if it was offered.'

He was quite still for another moment and then he turned, slowly, to glance at her still sitting primly on the chair in front of the desk.

She was one hell of a beautiful woman. The thought came from nowhere and he found it intensely irritating. Beautiful, but with an air of wary vulnerability one moment and steel-like hardness the next. Nothing about her seemed to add up and he was sure she was keeping plenty from him—as far as skeletons in the cupboard went he wouldn't be surprised if she had several rooms full of them.

From all she had said it sounded as though the kid was nothing more than an appendage to her life; women like her should never have children of their own. It was a sweeping statement and he recognised it as such, which further irritated him.

Damn it all, he knew nothing about her and her private life was no concern of his. As long as she did her job, that was all he was interested in. The thought caught him, tightening his mouth still more. Anyone would think he was offering her the job and he still had two of the other applicants to see yet, one of whom appeared to be a second June—if that were possible.

'So, thank you for attending this interview, Mrs Allen, and we'll be in touch within a day or two.'

It was a clear dismissal and Kim rose immediately to her feet, only to find she didn't quite know what to do with the coffee cup.

'May I...?' He moved round the desk and again she felt that little curling in her insides as the sheer breadth and height of him dwarfed her. At five foot ten she wasn't used to feeling so tiny and it was disconcerting to say the least.

'Thank you.' As he reached for the coffee cup she was

careful not to let her fingers touch his although she couldn't for the life of her have explained why. He was so close now she caught the faintest whiff of delicious and probably wildly expensive aftershave, and the effect of it on her sensitised nerves was enough to make her take a hasty step backwards, almost falling over the chair behind her as she did so.

Great. That was all she needed. Wouldn't he just love it if she fell flat on her face in front of him? It was enough to put iron in her backbone and a tight smile on her face as she gathered up her bag and coat, and said steadily, 'Goodbye, Mr Kane. I'll wait to hear from you.' And they both knew exactly what his decision would be, didn't they? she added with silent bitterness.

'Goodbye, Mrs Allen.' There was a bite to the words; he had obviously noticed her involuntary recoil and hadn't appreciated it, Kim thought wretchedly, humiliation adding more depth to the colour staining her cheeks.

The two or three steps to the interconnecting door seemed like miles, but then she was outside in June West's office and Kim was amazed how utterly normal everything seemed. She had just endured one of the most—no, probably *the* most—unnerving experiences of her life and June West was sitting typing away at her word processor as though nothing had happened. But then she dealt with Lucas Kane every day of her life. The thought was astounding and Kim found herself looking at the other woman with new respect as she made her goodbyes and escaped to the lift.

What had made her say she would take the post if it was offered? As the lift whisked her silently downwards, Kim stared at her reflection in the mirrored wall in horror. Well, she knew why—filthy lucre! She gave a weak grin and the dark-eyed girl staring at her grinned back.

Not that her agreement was any cause for concern—

Lucas Kane was as likely to offer her the job as a trip to the moon. She nodded to the thought, faintly comforted but still trembling slightly.

She didn't know how anyone could survive working for such a man; he was too cold, too ruthless and overtly powerful to be human.

But the money *was* good. She shut her eyes for a second, thinking of the speed in which the remainder of Graham's debts could be settled if she had a salary like the one Lucas Kane had mentioned coming in every month. She and Melody could think about moving out of the grotty little bedsit they were forced to call home, and with a car—a BMW, he had said, hadn't he?—travelling would be a pleasure.

The lift glided to a halt and her eyes snapped open. Enough daydreaming. She stepped into the foyer and walked determinedly towards the far doors without looking to left or right. It wasn't going to happen—furthermore, she didn't *want* it to happen, she told herself firmly.

She would soon get another job and eventually, one day, she would be clear of the burden which hung like a great millstone round her neck. And she had Melody. She thought of her daughter's sweet little face and felt a flood of love sweep through her, dispelling all the heartache. Yes, she had Melody, and compared to Lucas Kane with all his millions that made her the richest woman on earth.

CHAPTER TWO

'So, ALL in all an unmitigated disaster, then?' Maggie said with forced brightness. 'Never mind, pet; on to the next one, eh? I get the car back from the garage tomorrow, so if you want to borrow it you can. Friday's the next interview, isn't it?'

Kim nodded. She was standing drinking a hasty cup of coffee in Maggie's ultra-modern kitchen before she left to pick up Melody from the Octopus club her daughter attended after school. 'At the accountant's on the corner of the street where I live, actually,' she answered with matching brightness, 'so I shan't need the car. The accountant's would be much handier than Kane Electrical, travel-wise.'

'Absolutely.'

'And it's a small place—just three or four work there, I think—so it's bound to be friendlier than a big firm like Kane's.'

'Definitely.'

'Oh, Maggie.' Kim put down her flamboyant mug painted with enormous red cherries abruptly and stared into her friend's bright blue eyes. 'All that money, and a car and *everything*.'

'Don't forget Lucas Kane goes with the deal.' Maggie was trying to find something positive to say about the lost chance of the century.

'I could put up with him,' Kim answered miserably. 'If it meant being able to move out of the bedsit and get somewhere with a garden for Melody I could put up with just about *anything*.'

'I know.' Maggie put a sympathetic hand on Kim's arm

for a moment. 'But anyone has only got to see you two together for a minute to know that Melody has something all the money in the world can't buy. There's an awful lot of kids with gardens and a nursery full of toys who have rotten childhoods, lass, with parents who don't give a damn.'

Maggie's Northern accent was always at its strongest when she was in earnest about something, and now Kim smiled into the round homely face as she said, 'Thanks, Maggie. You're one in a million.'

'Just repeat that in Pete's ear, would you? *Loudly!*'

Pete was Maggie's boyfriend of five years' standing who was incredibly inventive in avoiding any mention of commitment and settling down, much to Maggie's increasing exasperation. He worked as a stockbroker—a successful one, by all accounts—and occupied the flat above Maggie's, which was how the two of them had first met.

'I thought you were going to have a chat with him over the weekend? Lay it on the line about how you feel?' Kim said quietly, forgetting her own troubles for a moment as she looked into Maggie's sky-blue gaze. Pete commuted into London every day and arrived back at the flat well after eight each night, so any serious talking was always left until the weekends.

'I was.' Maggie shrugged her meaty shoulders disconsolately. 'But he wasn't feeling well—a touch of flu, I think—and I was snowed under with work anyway, so it perhaps wasn't the right time.'

Maggie was an interior designer and her star was rising in the career sense if not in her lovelife.

'He doesn't know how lucky he is, that's the trouble,' Kim said stoutly, finishing the last of the coffee in one gulp and placing the mug on Maggie's gleaming worktop.

'I've been thinking the same thing myself,' Maggie agreed wryly. 'Working from home is great in all sorts of ways but he knows I'm always here, no matter what, just waiting for him to come back from the City. The way he carries on sometimes, you'd think he was a Viking returning from a far distant land—he's such a drama queen! In his opinion, he's the high-flyer taking chances, on the cutting edge and all that, and I'm good old dependable Maggie with nothing to do but get ready with his pipe and slippers.'

'The short, sharp shock treatment might wake him up, if you can think of something not too life-threatening,' Kim advised with a grin. 'I'm sure he does love you, Maggie.'

'Ah, but how much, lass—that's the sixty-four dollar question, isn't it? I'm getting on for thirty; I can't wait around for ever!'

'I must go; Melody will be out soon.' Kim gave Maggie a quick hug and made for the door. 'Ring me later if you fancy a chat.'

'Even if it's just to moan about Pete?'

'Course. What else are friends for?'

Kim found herself sprinting the last hundred yards or so along the cold streets to the school, although there was no need; she was in plenty of time. She had always made sure—no matter how hectic or difficult her day or how heavy her workload—that either she or Maggie was there before time to pick up Melody.

Melody's huge, thickly lashed brown eyes were searching for her the second her daughter walked out of the school doors, and as the small face lit up and a little red-mittened hand waved frantically Kim felt a lump in her throat at the unabashed love on the tiny face so like her own.

'Mummy! Mummy!' Melody fairly flew across the playground and into Kim's waiting arms. 'Guess what? I'm going to be Mary in the Nativity and have a white dress and tinsel in my hair. Mrs Jones picked me specially.'

'That's wonderful, darling.'

'She said she can trust me not to be silly,' Melody continued solemnly. 'Cory Chambers was *very* silly today; she stuck a crayon up her nose and Mrs Jones couldn't get it down and Cory was crying her head off. Mrs Jones had to get her mummy.'

The chatter continued during the ten-minute walk to their bedsit, situated in a terraced street which was grim by any standards. A young married couple and several students occupied the other four bedsits the narrow, three-storey house contained, with a shared bathroom for all occupants on the top floor next to Kim's room.

The fact that the bathroom was right next door for Melody and that their elevated position cut out the possibility of noisy neighbours overhead were two small advantages in their somewhat miserable surroundings, but Kim fought a constant war against mould and damp, ancient plumping and poor lighting. It wasn't so bad in the summer, but the two winters they had spent at the house had been abysmal.

Kim had made their home as bright and attractive as she could with the minimum of expenditure, making bright red curtains and a matching duvet cover and cushions for the bed-settee she shared with Melody, and scattering several rugs over the threadbare carpet, but nothing could hide the general run-down ambience of the old building.

Once home, and with Melody settled in front of the fire with a glass of milk and a biscuit, happily watching her favourite TV programme, Kim set about preparing the evening meal. But in spite of all her efforts to the contrary she found she was constantly replaying every minute of the interview earlier that day over and over in her mind.

It had been a travesty. Her eyes narrowed and she sliced a hapless carrot with uncharacteristic savageness. From the second her eyes had met those of Lucas Kane in the reception area she hadn't stood a chance. The moment she had seen who was seated behind that desk she should have turned right round and marched out with her head held high. Instead... She gritted her teeth and another carrot met the same fate as the first.

Instead she had sat there and answered his barbed questions as though she wanted his precious job, and let him walk all over her in the process.

No—no, she hadn't, she argued in the next instant. He hadn't had it all his own way, and besides, she *did* want the job. She wanted it so much she ached with it—or, rather, she wanted what the position as secretary to the chairman and managing director of Kane Electrical would do for Melody, for them both.

But it wasn't going to happen. She added two pieces of chicken breast to the vegetables and popped the casserole in the dilapidated oven the bedsit boasted. And in spite of the huge financial rewards it was probably just as well. She couldn't even begin to imagine herself working for Lucas Kane.

At eight that evening, when the telephone rang in the hall downstairs and Juliana—one of the students—banged on Kim's door to say a Mr Lucas of Kane Electrical was asking for her, Kim found herself having to do just that very thing.

'This is Mrs Allen.' She didn't like the fact that her voice was so breathless but hoped he would put it down to the fact that she lived on the top floor—something Juliana had apparently pointed out to him, according to the raven-haired Italian girl.

'Lucas Kane, Mrs Allen.' The deep husky tones were just as compelling over the telephone and she could just picture him, eyes like silver ice and mouth a hard line in the darkly attractive face, sitting at that massive desk in what must now be a deserted office block. Not that he had to be there, of course, she amended silently. He could be calling her from home, wherever that was. 'I hope I'm not interrupting anything—you don't have guests?'

Guests? Once she and Melody were ensconced in the limited space within the bedsit, there was barely room to swing a cat, Kim thought drily. 'No, Mr Kane, I don't have guests.' Her voice was better this time; less of the Marilyn Monroe and more of a Katharine Hepburn briskness to it.

'Good.' It was cold and crisp, very much like the man himself. 'I'm ringing you to offer you the job, Mrs Allen,' he said, without any preamble. 'If you haven't changed your mind, of course.'

'I... You—' Pull yourself together, woman, she told herself silently. He's obviously looking for a secretary who can string two words together! 'That's wonderful, Mr Kane,' she managed faintly.

'Then you accept?'

'Yes—yes, I do, and thank you. Thank you very much indeed.' She forced herself to stop babbling, realising she had gone from one extreme to the other, and took a long breath before she said more slowly, 'When would you like me to start, Mr Kane?'

'Well, that was one of the points in your favour, Mrs Allen, the fact that you can begin immediately,' he said coolly. 'June is understandably anxious to join her fiancé as soon as she can and oversee the arrangements, the wedding being in the spring, but even allowing for the possibility you are an exceptionally quick learner—' did she detect a note of covert sarcasm there, Kim wondered, or was she getting paranoid about this man? '—it will take several weeks to pick up all the strings.'

'You want me to start tomorrow?' she asked with a calm she was far from feeling.

'I was going to suggest Monday, to give you time to make any provision for your daughter which might be necessary, but if you are able to come into the office tomorrow that would be excellent. June normally arrives about nine-ish, so any time after that would be fine.'

There was no trace of emotion or feeling in his voice and the lack of humanity was disconcerting, to say the least. As his personal assistant-cum-secretary, she was going to be working very closely with this intimidating machine—could she handle it? Kim asked herself frantically, before answering in the same instant, Don't be silly, of course you can handle it. You can't miss the chance of a lifetime through sheer cowardice.

'I'll be there, Mr Kane,' Kim said steadily.

'Good. I'll get Personnel to draw up a contract and arrange for a car to be delivered some time tomorrow so you can have it to drive home. Any particular colour you'd like?'

She almost said, Colour? before she bit the word back, but her hands were beginning to shake and her stomach was swirling with a mixture of amazement and delight at how suddenly her circumstances were changing and bone-chilling shock at her temerity. 'I don't know,' she said dazedly. 'This is all rather sudden.'

'Has your daughter got a favourite colour?' The deep, dark voice was as expressionless as ever, but the content of the question totally threw Kim in view of the robot asking it.

'Blue,' she faltered weakly.

'Just as well it's not shocking pink—BMW might have objected,' came the dry response. 'Blue it is, then, and I'll see a child's seat is fitted, of course. Goodnight, Mrs Allen.'

'Goodnight, and thank you for letting me know so promptly,' she said quickly, her head spinning.

'A pleasure.' It was soft and smooth, and although Kim told herself his reply was just a formal nicety, something in the silky tones sent a trickle of awareness down her spine.

He would be one sexy customer in bed. The thought—coming from nowhere as it did—horrified Kim so much it was just as well the phone had gone dead at the other end because she was quite unable to speak or move for a good thirty seconds.

Was she mad? she asked herself as she replaced the receiver with elaborate carefulness and then put both hands to her burning cheeks. Lucas Kane was her new boss and that last thought had been inappropriate to say the least. And machines weren't sexy. Powerful maybe, frightening sometimes, and certainly cold and efficient, but definitely not sexy.

She stood for a moment more and then, as her agitation subsided slightly and the full knowledge of what the new job package would mean swept over her, she took the stairs two at a time, bursting into the bedsit and doing something unheard of—waking Melody from a deep sleep and dancing round the room with her daughter's tiny body held tight in her arms.

The next morning was one of frosty brilliance, and when Kim awoke to a crystal-bright world and gazed out over the white sparkling rooftops as she fixed a hot drink for herself and Melody her heart was singing.

This was a new shiny beginning; even the weather confirmed it. She would start looking for a new place to live—a small ground-floor flat with a garden, maybe, or even a little house—this very weekend. She was going to be earning a small fortune; she could soon pay off the remaining debts, as long as she was careful, and then her life would be her own again. No more robbing Peter to pay Paul, no more working out how to make a pound stretch into two or three—oh, life was *wonderful*.

Once she had got Melody off to sleep again the night before she had phoned Maggie with the good news. Maggie had immediately offered to pop round early the next morning and take Melody to school, so Kim could arrive at Kane Electrical in plenty of time—the buses being unreliable at the best of times—and Kim had gratefully accepted her friend's kind offer.

So it was that Kim arrived outside the huge building just as June West drew into the 'Reserved for the secretary of the managing director' spot, and the two women walked into Reception together.

'Nervous?'

June was smiling sympathetically as she spoke and her voice was warm, and Kim smiled back weakly as she answered, 'A little. Well, a lot, really. My previous job wasn't anything like as high-powered as this one.'

'Don't worry, you'll be fine.' June was watching her closely and now, as the two women entered the lift and the doors glided shut, she added in a low tone, 'I shouldn't really be telling you this but there were dozens after the position, you know. Some were better-qualified than you, some were more experienced, but Lucas chose you and that means, as far as he's concerned, you are the best for the job.'

Kim knew June had meant her words to be uplifting but they had the opposite effect. All she could manage, as the lift doors opened to disgorge them into the exalted upper sanctum, was, 'You call him Lucas? Not to his face, surely?' She hadn't got Lucas Kane down as being on first-name terms with his secretary somehow.

'Sure.' June grinned at her conspiratorially. 'You'll find him quite different to the public image, once you get to know him, and he hates to stand on ceremony in private. Of course, in front of other colleagues and business clients, it's Mr Kane and Miss West, or in your case Mrs Allen.'

'Right.' Oh, help!

'He's a good boss to work for, Kim, take it from me,'

June continued easily as they walked along the corridor. 'I wouldn't have stayed ten years otherwise.'

'How…how old is he?' Kim asked nervously.

'Thirty-seven. He took over the business when he was only twenty-five. His father, who founded the firm, got sick—cancer, I think, leukaemia or something to do with the blood, anyway—and had to have months and months of treatment. Lucas stepped in; he'd been with the firm for four years, since leaving university, but when he took charge he did so well, apparently, that his father decided to retire and let him take over permanently, and since then the business has gone from strength to strength. It was only a tenth of its present size when I started.'

June opened the door into her office, lowering her voice as she glanced towards the interconnecting door, and added, 'He's got a reputation for having the Midas touch, and admittedly he does have brilliant business acumen, but his competitors don't see the endless hours he puts into the business while they're off swanning round a golf course or having holidays in the Caribbean. He deserves every little bit of success he's had. I don't know anyone who works so hard.'

'I appreciate the accolade, June, but just in case the tenor changes I think I'd better point out the cleaners seem to have knocked the switch on the intercom again.'

The voice was dry, very dry, but as June glanced at her Kim saw the older woman's face was quite unabashed and her expression was reflected in her voice when June said, 'Whoops, that was a near thing, Lucas. Another minute and your ears might have begun to burn.'

'My ears are incapable of burning, June, as you very well know.' It was even drier. 'Do I take it Mrs Allen is with you?'

'Yes, she's here,' June confirmed quickly.

'Then I would like a word with her, before you start

addling her brain with a hundred and one facts,' the dark
voice said evenly. 'And a cup of black coffee, when you're
ready.'

'Coming right up.' June flicked the switch on the intercom and smiled breezily at Kim as she indicated for her to
go through into Lucas Kane's office, and Kim found herself
thinking—as she had done at the interview the afternoon
before—that she would never, ever—not in a million
years—*ever* be able to mirror the relaxed approach June
apparently had in dealing with her formidable boss.

She quickly slipped out of her coat, smoothed down her
already sleek and shining hair, caught in a neat and somewhat severe pleat at the back of her head, and took a deep
breath as she walked across the room and opened the door
into Lucas Kane's office.

'Good morning.' The devastating silver-grey eyes were
waiting for her and in spite of all her preparation for this
moment Kim's heart bounded in her chest. 'You haven't
changed your mind, then?'

'Changed my mind?' She stared at the big figure seated
behind the desk in surprise. 'Of course not, Mr Kane. I told
you I would be here this morning.'

'And you always do what you promise?' he asked
smoothly, his pearly gaze narrowing on her flushed face.

'Yes, I do.'

There was a slight bristle in the words which Lucas registered with hidden amusement, but his voice betrayed
nothing of what he was feeling when he said, 'Good. We'll
get along just fine in that case, Mrs Allen.'

He rose from behind the massive desk as he spoke and
Kim forced herself to show no reaction at all when he
perched himself easily on the side of it, the hard lean body
giving the impression of a coiled spring just waiting to
pounce.

'The car, a blue BMW, will be delivered before four
o'clock.' His tone was steady now, almost bored. 'That will

give ample time for you to be able to familiarise yourself
with the controls and ask any questions you feel relevant.'

'Thank you.' She didn't know what else to say.

'I trust your daughter will be satisfied with the colour
when she sees it.'

Kim glanced sharply at him then but the sardonic attractive face was expressionless, as was his voice when he
continued, 'Over the next few weeks you will learn how
this office works and what makes me tick, Mrs Allen.'

Her wide open eyes blinked once but she didn't make
the mistake of rushing into speech and the carved lips
twitched a little. 'Let me save a little time and lay down
some ground rules which I'm sure will benefit us both?'

It was in the form of a rhetorical question but Kim nodded nevertheless, it seemed to be expected somehow.

'As I mentioned yesterday, I expect—*demand*—absolute
loyalty from those close to me; anything less is unacceptable. As my secretary and personal assistant, you will be
privy to all manner of confidential information, both with
regard to business and my private life. I expect you to be
unconditionally discreet in both areas.'

He had nodded at her to sit down when he had settled
himself on the edge of the desk and Kim was thankful of
it now; she felt utterly overwhelmed by the sheer magnetism of the man who was now her boss. Her *boss*. Her
stomach turned right over and she swallowed hard. 'Of
course, Mr Kane.'

'Lucas.' He leant back slightly, the blue-black of his hair
accentuated by the white sunlight behind him. 'If you are
serious about working with me, the second thing you have
to learn is that all formality stops at that door.' He nodded
to the interconnecting door behind her. 'You are my eyes
and ears in this organisation and beyond, a valuable second
opinion and ally who must be completely frank within the
confines of these four walls.'

'And if my opinion doesn't fit in with yours?' she asked with a careful neutrality that hid her jangling nerves.

He said nothing for a second, just looking at her with piercing eyes, and then he smiled. The first real smile she had seen. 'I'm not looking for you to agree with me, necessarily,' he said quietly, 'but if you do disagree I expect your comments to be logical and well informed. I have enough sycophantic boot-lickers around already; I don't need another one, Kim.'

It was the first time he had said her Christian name and, ridiculous though she told herself it was, it did something strange to her insides. Something she didn't care to examine. *He was too close.* The thought came from nowhere and she told herself sharply she was acting like a skittish schoolgirl, not a mature woman of twenty-six.

To combat the weakness she forced herself to smile back, her tone light as she said, 'Dare I ask if I can remind you of that in the future?'

The smile grew, turning the aggressively male face of hard angles and planes into a more mellow whole, and Kim watched, fascinated.

'I have the feeling you will do so with or without my blessing,' he said lazily, before levering himself off the desk in one easy movement and seating himself in the massive leather chair again. 'Observe much, say little and keep your wits about you during the next few weeks, Kim, and you'll do just fine. It's nice to have you aboard.'

'Thank you.' It was a clear dismissal and Kim rose a trifle flusteredly, hoping her tension didn't show. He was the most disturbing man she had ever met, but she had to find a way of coping with how she felt—and fast. This job was too fantastic an opportunity to blow.

It was that thought which enabled her to leave Lucas's office with measured steps, her blonde head high and her face deadpan.

It would be all right, she assured herself, standing aside

to let June pass into the Holy of Holies with the coffee. She had June to soften her absorption into the role of secretary to Lucas Kane and the other woman would be around for some weeks yet. After that…

Her heart began to thud and she clucked her tongue at herself, annoyed at her nervousness. After that she would be just what he wanted her to be—an efficient, cool, capable machine who ran his office like clockwork. *She could do this.* If nothing else, her time with Graham, not to mention the searing aftermath, had shown her she had hidden resources she had never dreamt of.

When she thought of that nightmare funeral, which had occurred the day after she had found out she was not only destitute but thousands and thousands of pounds in debt, she knew nothing could ever be as bad again.

But she had come through that, and not crawling on her belly, either—she'd carved out a reasonable life for herself and Melody and it was going to get better and better from this point on. She was in charge of her own destiny—hers and Melody's—and the vow she had made standing in the pouring rain at the side of the newly dug grave still held good. Never again would she put her trust in any one man; she had learnt a hard lesson but she'd learnt it well. Men said one thing with their lips but their mind was thinking something else. They could be sweetness and light in company—with everyone else—but in the privacy of their own home turn into the devil incarnate.

She was autonomous now—blessedly, gloriously autonomous—and nothing, *nothing*, would ever persuade her to be anything else. And this job would ensure her material security in a way she had never imagined; it was her chance of a lifetime.

Secretary to Lucas Kane? Kim glanced at the closed door, beyond which she could hear the low murmur of voices. She was going to be the best secretary he'd ever had or die in the attempt!

CHAPTER THREE

OVER the next few weeks Kim worked as she had never worked before. She made copious notes of everything June told her, taking reams of paper home each night and sitting up until well past midnight, memorising anything and everything which was relevant. She acquainted herself with every file, every company, every individual who played a role in Lucas Kane's business life until she had more facts and figures in her head than June did.

One of Melody's schoolfriends lived directly opposite her daughter's school and Kim came to an arrangement with the child's mother that in return for the payment of a small fee she could drop Melody off at just gone eight every day, enabling the blue BMW to purr into Kane Electrical's car park every morning before half-past eight.

Kim had imagined, the first day, that it would be just her and possibly the caretaker in the building, but Lucas's sleek, champagne-coloured Aston Martin was already in residence when she had pulled up and it continued to be so every morning.

He had come to the door of his office on her early arrival and gazed quizzically at her for a moment or two, but beyond a request for one of the endless cups of coffee he consumed all day had made no comment.

Christmas had come and gone, and Kim had gulped slightly at the size of her very generous Christmas box from Lucas in the form of a cheque, and in the second week in January she and Melody had moved into the small but charming two-bedroomed cottage she had found not far from her daughter's school.

And then the Monday of the third week was upon her, the first day June wouldn't be there to cushion her from any minor panics, the other woman having left for Scotland the previous weekend. And Kim found she was as nervous as a child on its first day at school.

She'd gone to extra trouble with her appearance, the clothing allowance having enabled her to buy a new wardrobe consisting of several stylish, neatly tailored suits, blouses and accessories which perfectly projected the image Lucas Kane's secretary needed to give, and Kim knew the dove-grey suit and salmon silk blouse complemented her English peaches and cream colouring.

Nevertheless, her soft brown eyes were wide and faintly anxious as she checked the coiled braid on the back of her head, her thick straight fringe just brushing the tops of her fine eyebrows.

'Nothing has changed in the last forty-eight hours,' she told the efficient-looking reflection softly. 'You've been working for him for the last week or so with June doing little more than observing; you can handle anything now.'

Kim had to remind herself of that last comforting assurance in the next minute or two.

Over the last weeks she had slipped into the pattern of serving Lucas coffee as soon as she arrived in the office, but when, after the normal customary polite knock, Kim opened the door, it wasn't the usual immaculately attired and perfectly groomed tycoon she had grown accustomed to who looked up from his desk.

Lucas had obviously been asleep until she had woken him, and now, as he straightened and peered at her from bleary eyes, Kim's heartbeat went haywire.

It wasn't the fact that he hadn't shaved or brushed his hair, or that his dishevelled appearance bore evidence to the fact that he had slept in his clothes that had her insides turning cartwheels.

At some time during the last hours he had discarded his
suit jacket along with his tie, and now his open shirt revealed a deep V of tanned flesh sprinkled with dark curling
body hair and a muscled—devastatingly muscled—male
chest of Olympic athlete proportions.

He worked out. He very clearly worked out. Kim was
glued to the spot, the tray with the coffee and plate of
biscuits wobbling dangerously in her hand. And he was...
Well, he was something else, she admitted with silent
shock. Clothed, he was pretty intimidating and all male, but
partly clothed... No wonder June had told her that the fast
car went with equally fast, glamorous women and a love
'em and leave 'em personal life where work—always—
came first.

'Not that it seems to put them off,' June had murmured
confidentially. 'Of course, the circle he moves in are all of
the same mind, I guess, so that helps. Lucas has never been
one for the dumb blonde type female; he goes for brains
as well as beauty. The last one was a lawyer, the one before
that a mogul with her own business—they all seem to find
him irresistible.'

She hadn't made any comment at the time although she
had silently told herself that irresistible was definitely *not*
a word that came to mind when she thought of Lucas Kane,
but now, if nothing else, she could appreciate what drew
and held such women.

Taken off his guard like this, and with his office mode
in abeyance for once, she was seeing the raw animal magnetism she had sensed once or twice—well, a lot more than
once or twice, she admitted ruefully—in all its deadly
power.

'Hell, what's the time?' The silver eyes were clearing
even as he spoke and granite was replacing the faint smoky
hue that had been so stunningly sexy.

'Eight-thirty.' It was succinct but all she could manage until her hormones sorted themselves out.

'Is that coffee? You're an angel.' He leant back in the chair and stretched magnificent muscles before raking back his hair, none of which did Kim's equilibrium any favours. 'I've been here most of the weekend; the Clarkson deal blew up in our face and needed some quality time.'

'Right.' Kim nodded in what she hoped was an informed, efficient sort of way and wondered if he was aware he was half naked. If he was it clearly didn't bother him.

She placed the coffee and biscuits on the desk in front of him and prayed her face wasn't as flushed as she feared it was.

'But I've got it nailed.' He reached for one of the biscuits and ate it in a hungry bite before reaching for another.

'When did you eat last?' she asked carefully.

'Eat?' The crystal-bright eyes that could be so piercingly intent were vague. 'I don't remember. Saturday, I think.'

'Fancy some bacon sandwiches?'

'Bacon sandwiches?' He stared at her interestedly. 'Don't tell me you can provide those at a moment's notice, Kim?'

'Almost.' She was fighting sexual arousal and it made her voice stiff. 'There's a little man on the corner who comes every morning in his mobile and does a roaring trade, apparently. Bacon sandwiches are his speciality.'

'Then I'd like six rounds from your little man,' Lucas said promptly, 'with lashings of brown sauce.'

She inclined her head, as she imagined the estimable June would have done in the same circumstances, and forced herself to turn and walk towards the door. 'I'll be ten minutes or so,' she said evenly over her shoulder and she didn't look back.

She was fifteen minutes, and when she knocked for the second time that morning on Lucas's door and walked into his office, her boss had transformed himself—courtesy of the small bathroom and dressing room, which were part of his executive suite—into his usual cool and impeccable self. But in spite of the fresh charcoal suit and pale blue shirt with matching tie, all Kim could see was a mental picture of acres and acres of finely honed muscled flesh and it was disconcerting, to say the least.

It didn't help that his hair was still slightly damp from the shower and his freshly shaved face more relaxed than usual, either, and the hot prickle of overt sexual awareness that had hit her so forcefully earlier didn't seem to want to die the death she was willing on it.

'Six rounds of doorsteps with what looks like a pound of bacon in them,' she said as expressionlessly as she could. 'Eat them while they're hot.' She handed him the plate as she spoke.

'You sound like my mother.'

His *mother*? She narrowed her eyes and smiled sweetly. 'Don't tell me you are one of those men who have a mother fixation,' she said coolly before she thought too much about it and didn't dare voice the tart retort which had sprung to mind.

'I don't think so.' He was eyeing her with what could only be termed a glint, but a glint of what Kim wasn't sure. 'My mother is a wonderful woman and ideally suited to my father, but...no, I don't think so.' He took a bite of one of the sandwiches and closed his eyes in ecstasy.

'How come I haven't had bacon sandwiches from your little man before?' he asked almost petulantly.

'Because you didn't ask?' she suggested daringly.

The silver eyes fastened on her, pinning her to the spot, and Lucas smiled slowly. 'I only have to ask?' he drawled lazily.

She might have known she had no chance of winning in a war of words with him! Kim was disturbingly aware that something had shifted in the last few minutes, something that had been bubbling away under the surface from the first moment she had laid eyes on Lucas Kane—something that couldn't, mustn't, have expression. 'I'll get you another cup of coffee.' She had turned and swept out of the room before he had time to take another bite.

Lucas smiled faintly to himself. There was more, much more, to his efficient, beautiful new secretary than met the eye; he had known that from the beginning. And was that why he had been tempted to choose Kim above other more qualified, experienced candidates?

The thought didn't sit well with him and the smile turned into a frown. He had chosen Kim Allen because she was the most suitable applicant—qualifications and experience weren't necessarily the be-all and end-all of a working relationship, he told himself sharply. There had to be a spark, a cutting edge, a quality that was undefinable but which told you any association would be healthy and productive without becoming dull or boring. He had never wanted a mindless android who wouldn't say boo to a goose. That was why he had chosen Kim. And her qualifications were pretty good too, as was her experience.

June had had it—they had enjoyed some very real altercations in their time, he assured himself firmly, ignoring the little voice of honesty which suggested he was comparing chalk to cheese.

He was suddenly uncomfortable with his thoughts and, reaching for another sandwich, having finished the first, he turned his mind to the Clarkson file sitting in front of him, dismissing all further thoughts of Kim with the single-minded ruthlessness that had made Kane Electrical so successful in the last decade.

It took Kim a good deal longer to get her unregenerate thoughts under lock and key, but once she had succeeded she determined they wouldn't escape again. Lucas Kane could prance around naked if he so desired and she wouldn't turn a hair, she told herself on the drive home that evening.

She had to admit he had a certain something, a darkly seductive something—in fact it was a relief to acknowledge it and bring it out into the open, she assured herself firmly. He *was* a compellingly attractive man—most powerful, wealthy men had an aura that set them apart from the crowd—but it didn't make them easy to live with or likeable.

And she didn't have to like him; as long as she could respect his business acumen and flair and enjoy her work, that was all she wanted. His lifestyle and the way he conducted his personal relationships was absolutely no concern of hers; the fact that he embodied everything she most disliked in a man in that area didn't mean she couldn't work with him. He saw her as part of the office machinery, not a woman, and that made all the difference.

She was well satisfied with her reasoning by the time she drew up outside the school gates and parked the car, walking down the concrete drive and standing to one side of the big wooden doors as the first desultory snowflakes began to fall out of a laden sky.

By the time Melody emerged with one or two other children—the teacher standing just behind them and checking each child had its respective escort—the snow was coming down in thick fat white flakes that sent the children into transports of delight.

'Mummy, it's *really* snowing!' Melody danced up to her, her small face alight. 'Can we build a snowman in the garden?'

'Maybe tomorrow, if it snows enough,' Kim agreed warmly. The cottage had a delightful garden with a large lawn surrounded by mature trees and shrubs, and Melody had already commandeered a small corner of it, announcing she was going to plant her own herb garden in the spring.

She would, too, Kim thought fondly as they walked to the car. Anything she set her mind to, Melody did; her small daughter was bubbling over with confidence and vitality and thankfully had no memory of the last terrible months Graham had put them through before he had died.

She refused to dwell on thoughts of her late husband, concentrating on Melody and asking her small daughter about her day, but once Melody was in bed and the cottage was quiet she found the memories flooding in in spite of all her efforts to shut them out.

She had thought she loved Graham—she had been *sure* she loved him—but the old adage that said you never knew someone until you lived with them had certainly been true in her husband's case, she reflected bitterly.

The handsome, bright, only son of aged doting parents, Graham had been spoilt outrageously from the cradle. In spite of their fairly limited means, Graham's parents had endeavoured to give their charismatic offspring everything he wanted, even financing the one-man business he had set up after finishing university, although it had taken every last penny they had.

She hadn't been aware of that at the time; she hadn't been aware of many things which had come to light after Graham's death.

She hadn't known he had a drink problem at university—everyone drank, it was part of the culture, and Graham had been adept at hiding his addiction from her. And by the time it became apparent he was an alcoholic she had been pregnant with Melody and desperate to make her marriage work for the sake of their unborn baby.

Graham's business had failed almost immediately—it couldn't have done anything else with the lack of time and effort he had put into it—and with his parents unable to bail him out he had started borrowing from all and sundry, using his compelling charm and attractiveness to get him what he needed. He had always had the ability to be irresistible when he had put his mind to it.

Kim glanced up suddenly from the task of darning the hole in the pocket of Melody's school coat.

Irresistible. The word had suddenly switched on a light in her mind and now she understood why she was thinking of Graham after months of being able to shut him out. 'They all seem to find him irresistible.' Those were the very words June had used about Lucas.

Kim's soft mouth straightened into a hard line and her dark brown eyes narrowed unseeingly across the cosy sitting room. 'They' all might find Lucas Kane irresistible, but this was one female who had received very powerful antibodies against such a disease, she told herself savagely, acknowledging in the same instant that the little episode in Lucas's office that morning had bothered her more than she had admitted.

He was the first man who had even remotely stirred her sexual awareness since Graham had died, but now she had recognised the fact and the danger it represented she would be on her guard against herself twenty-four hours a day. It wasn't that she thought he would be interested in her in a personal way—she almost laughed out loud at the thought of the ruthless and focused Lucas Kane harbouring romantic inclinations towards his secretary—but she didn't want to be attracted to any man, ever again, and certainly not one cast in Graham's mould.

She had never told anyone about those last awful twelve months with Graham, the humiliations she had suffered at his hands, and she never would. She didn't have to. She was answerable to no one and that was the way she liked it. Melody was the only important thing in her life and, thanks to this new job—she couldn't bring herself to say

thanks to Lucas Kane—she was going to be able to give
her daughter the kind of lifestyle she hadn't imagined was
remotely in her grasp just a few months ago. And nothing—
nothing—must interfere with that.

She nodded sharply to herself, her eyes focusing once
more on the small red coat in her hands, and as she set to
again with renewed vigour her lips were still drawn uncharacteristically tight.

The next morning there were several inches of snow and
the world had been transformed into a winter wonderland,
much to Melody's delight, but the BMW regally ignored
such trifles as snow-packed roads and icy conditions.

Once Kim had dropped Melody off and was on her way
to work she found herself thinking, as she had done more
than once in the last few weeks, how fortunate she was to
have such a powerful and comfortable car at her disposal.
No more struggling along glassy pavements with wet feet
or sitting in a cold bus which had arrived late and was filled
with the musty smell of damp humanity.

As usual Lucas was already in his office when she arrived. She had the feeling that if she went into work at five
in the morning she would still find him there.

She assumed the routine the hiccup yesterday had interrupted, taking his coffee into him once she had divested
herself of her coat and quickly smoothed her hair in her
small cloakroom.

'Good morning, Kim.' He didn't raise his head from the
report he was studying as he spoke and his voice was polite
and cool.

Kim answered in the same vein, placing the tray on the
desk and forcing herself to walk smoothly out of the office
without allowing her glance to linger on the dark bent head
and harshly carved lines of his face, but, annoyingly, she
found her heart was beating a tattoo as she sat down in

front of her word processor and the hand that raised her coffee to her lips was shaking slightly.

She was glad they had reverted to the businesslike working relationship of the previous weeks, of course she was, she told herself silently. So why did she feel his cool remoteness was almost like a slap across the face? *Ridiculous.* She nodded irritably to the thought. She was being absolutely ridiculous—it must be the time of the month or something.

She grimaced to herself, drank the coffee in several burningly hot gulps and got down to work.

At five past ten Kim put through a call from the managing director of Clarkson International, and at ten past Lucas put his head round the door. 'One of those tapes on your desk is a breakdown of the Clarkson contract so far. Concentrate on that first, would you, Kim? I need it for twelve. And we're lunching with them today at one, by the way, so book a table for four at Fontella's.'

Kim stared at him, her mind racing. 'Do you mean you want me to accompany you?' she asked politely, her face and voice hiding all signs of agitation.

'Yes, and you'll need to bring your notebook and pencil, and get a financial report from Accounts. We might need that.' He was totally in work mode, his distant voice indicating he was thinking about several things at once. She had noticed that about him before; it was one of the many accomplishments he had that added to the notion he wasn't quite human.

'Right.' She nodded efficiently and then, once the door had closed again, sat staring vacantly across the room. A business lunch with clients, that was all it was. She could handle this. This sort of thing was going to happen time and time again so she might as well get used to it.

The breakdown was on Lucas's desk at half-past eleven and Kim was waiting—outwardly serene and inwardly disturbed and uptight—at twelve-thirty when he buzzed her to say they were leaving. Her stomach muscles had tightened as the deep dark voice came over the intercom, but when he emerged from his office a few moments later she was all cucumber-cool efficiency.

'We're meeting them at Fontella's so I'd like to get there a few minutes early.' He took her arm as he spoke, ushering her out of the door with his usual fast, capable way of doing things. She caught a whiff of the expensive aftershave he wore, the feel of his height and breadth all around her as they entered the lift at the end of the corridor, and it was then she carefully moved away and put a little space between them.

'What's the matter?'

'I'm sorry?' She stared at him as he leant against the carpeted panelling and looked at her quizzically, but she couldn't stop her cheeks flushing with colour. She had thought her cautious withdrawal had been sufficiently diplomatic and discreet to be unnoticed, but she might have know that razor-sharp brain would have detected it.

'You didn't like me touching you,' he stated evenly, his narrowed eyes like twin points of silver light. 'Why? Is it me or are you the same with all men?'

Any other man, *any other man*, might have registered her unease but wouldn't have confronted her on it. The thought hit Kim at the same time as the hostility at his astute assessment of her, and her voice was icy when she said, in direct answer to the challenge, 'I don't like physical contact, as it happens.'

'I'll forgo the joke about your daughter being born through immaculate conception,' he drawled drily, 'and repeat my question. Do you have a problem with me, Kim? If so, it needs to be brought out into the open and dealt with. I'm not in the habit of jumping on unsuspecting females; neither do I believe in mixing work and pleasure. Is that plain enough for you?'

This was awful, horrific. Kim had never felt so embarrassed in her life. She stared at him and then as the lift glided gently to a halt she saw the gleam in his eyes. It could have been anger, it could have been irritation or a whole host of things, but to her utter humiliation she rather suspected it was dark amusement. And if nothing else it restored her fighting spirit in a way nothing else could have done.

'I really don't know what you are talking about,' she said with painful self-dignity. 'I merely stated that I don't like physical contact, that's all.'

'I don't consider taking your arm physical contact in any real meaning of the words.' It was cool, firm and completely without emotion. 'So you had better get used to it, okay? I'm not about to watch every movement I make in case I offend you, Kim, so get your head round that and save us both a lot of trouble.'

Her mouth had widened slightly in a little O of surprise and when the lift doors opened in the next instant and his cool hand cupped her elbow she offered no resistance at all. They were through Reception and out into the front car park within seconds, and he guided her over to the gleaming Aston Martin without speaking, opening the passenger door for her with a courtesy she suspected was entirely natural.

Kim sank into the luxurious confines of the powerful car and watched him helplessly as he walked round the sleek low bonnet. She hated him. She really hated him, she told herself bitterly. He was the most unfeeling, callous, hard brute of a man she had ever met—and that included Graham. No amount of money was worth this.

'Kim?'

She had continued staring straight ahead, her cheeks

burning, after he had slid into the car, and when after a long moment or two he spoke, very softly, her head jerked in surprise to meet the silver-grey of his eyes.

'I handled that very badly. I'm sorry,' Lucas said quietly.

If the ground had suddenly opened beneath them and engulfed the car she couldn't have been more surprised.

'You hit me on the raw,' he admitted softly. 'I didn't like being put in the position of feeling like some sexual pervert. I've never had that happen to me before.'

'Lucas, I...' She had gone all hot inside and had never felt more out of her depth. It wasn't just his apology, surprising though it was, but the disturbing fact that he was closer than he had ever been and his overall maleness was swamping her to a point where she felt breathless.

He was so big and dark and *masculine* and in this present mood, with his deep voice slightly husky and smoky and his amazing eyes intent on her face, the magnetism that was an intrinsic part of his dangerous attractiveness was heightened tenfold.

'Was it your marriage?' he asked, with a gentleness she would have sworn he was incapable of.

Oh, hell, what did she say now? She said the only thing she could in view of the fact that he had abased himself so utterly. 'Yes.' It was tight and stiff. 'It was my marriage.'

'I'm sorry.'

He really sounded as though he was, but, having turned to look through the windscreen once more, Kim didn't dare meet those devastating arctic eyes again. 'It's all right.' It was inane but all she could manage. 'Shouldn't we go now?'

'Did he hurt you? Physically, I mean?' There was a strange note in Lucas's voice and Kim wasn't to know her ruthless, cold, unemotional boss was in the grip of feelings new to him.

The silence stretched and lengthened until it was so taut

Kim felt she would either scream or faint. She did neither, merely saying, in a small, chilled little voice, 'I don't want to be rude but I can't discuss it, Lucas.'

She didn't expect him to let it go without a fight but he surprised her for the second time in as many minutes when he started the engine without another word, pulling out of the company car park with a savagery that made the car growl as he murmured, 'Without knowing any of the facts, and in direct variance to the notion that you shouldn't speak ill of the dead, I'd say you were well rid of the—' He stopped abruptly. 'You're well rid of Mr Allen,' he finished tightly.

How right he was. She gave a peculiar little laugh. 'I know it.'

'How did it happen?' For a moment she glanced at him, at the harsh set face frowning at the road ahead, uncertain of what he was asking. 'How did he die?' Lucas asked abruptly. 'Your application form merely stated "deceased".'

'It was an accident.' She didn't want to continue this.

She was aware of the piercing eyes flashing over her face although she was looking straight ahead again, and his voice had the smoky quality that was so disturbing when he said, 'Car?'

'No.' They were in mainstream traffic now but, in spite of their conversation, the frantic rush hour busyness and the fact that it had begun to snow again making the difficult driving conditions even more treacherous, all Kim was conscious of was hard male thighs just on the perimeter of her visions and firm capable tanned hands on the leather steering wheel. And the smell of him. Whatever aftershave he was using it should be banned as downright dangerous to a woman's state of mind, she told herself silently. But perhaps it wouldn't smell the same on anyone else.

'Graham cut an artery when he fell through a shop window.' A full thirty seconds had crept by in screaming expectation and Kim couldn't take the pressure any more. 'He was drunk,' she finished flatly.

'Usual occurrence?' The silver light moved over her briefly.

For a man who used words so sparingly he certainly made every one count, Kim thought resentfully. 'Yes,' she said hollowly.

'And now you want to talk about something else.'

She had wanted to talk about something else from the moment she had got into the car! Kim sucked in a shaky breath and kept her trembling hands tightly clasped in her lap. 'If you don't mind,' she said numbly.

Lucas nodded slowly. 'Tell me about your daughter.' And his cool voice didn't betray he was as surprised by the request as Kim was.

'Melody?' Kim was startled into glancing at him and he met her big brown eyes for a second, his own thick black lashes hiding his expression in the next instant.

'Unusual name. Your choice?' he asked easily.

The scent of his male warmth was unnerving her more and more in the close confines of the powerfully virile car, forcing her to acknowledge her own awareness of him with a tenacity she couldn't escape. 'It was a long labour, difficult.' She didn't add that Graham had been out on a drinking binge and had only arrived at the hospital the following morning. 'One of the nurses was very sweet to me; she was Jamaican. Her name was—'

'Melody.' He finished the sentence for her.

Kim nodded. 'But it suits Melody,' she said quietly. 'She's a happy little girl, always singing and laughing.'

There was a warmth—a sweetness—to Kim's voice when she spoke of her daughter that Lucas hadn't heard before, and suddenly he was the one who wanted to change the subject.

'I'm sure she is,' he said evenly. 'Now, let me just run through the prime objective of this meeting before we meet Jim Clarkson and his son.'

Kim listened quietly as he expounded further, but inside she was so churned up half of what he said flowed straight over her head.

She wished she'd never taken this job. In spite of the fabulous salary, the car, everything, she did so wish she'd never set foot in Kane Electrical. She had known where she was with Bob Curtis. He had been a slave-driver, and quite shameless about using people to his own advantage, but he had been fat and balding and middle-aged and hadn't had the interest to ask her one personal question in the two years she had worked for him. And he'd driven a family saloon that was as exciting as a jam sandwich.

Lucas shifted slightly in the black leather seat and she felt her nerves tighten.

And Bob's suits had been off the peg and more often than not creased into the bargain, and he would no more have worn a silk shirt than the man in the moon. Whereas Lucas... Even in bathing trunks he would still have that air of unlimited wealth about him.

The thought of Lucas in bathing trunks was enough to cause her cheeks to flush hotly, and she hoped he would assume it was the warmth of the car after the bitter chill outside if he noticed.

Lucas did notice, and the feeling he had experienced in the lift swept over him again with renewed vigour before he forced himself to relax. Okay, so she was as nervous as a cat on a hot tin roof, he told himself with silent savagery, but the devil alone only knew what had gone on in her marriage. At least the creep was dead. He breathed out slowly, narrowing his eyes at the wintry vista ahead as he forced himself to concentrate on the road conditions. She was his secretary. That was all she was. Her past only affected him in as much as it might interfere with the job she did for him. *That was all.*

The rest of the journey to the restaurant was conducted in a silence that wasn't at all comfortable, and by the time the Aston Martin nosed into the immaculate car park at the rear of Fontella's, Kim's nerves were stretched to breaking point. Lucas was out of the car and opening her door before Kim had a chance to move, and as she swung her legs on to the gravelled drive she took a long, deep, silent breath.

She knew of Fontella's but had never ventured within its hallowed walls. The prices began at unaffordable and rose skywards.

'Chin up.'

She hadn't been aware of Lucas's eyes on her as they had begun to walk towards the gracious wooden doors leading into the building, but now as she glanced at him he continued, 'Jim is a wily old bird but as down-to-earth a guy as you could wish to meet and his son is from the same mould. You'll like them.'

Probably, but it wasn't the thought of meeting the king-pins of Clarkson International that was bothering her. It was the big dark man at the side of her. For some reason he caused a chemical reaction in her mind and body that she didn't seem able to control with logic or will-power, and it was getting worse as time progressed, not better.

Kim did like Jim Clarkson and his son, Robert. They were astute businessmen and as single-minded as Lucas when it came to any issues linked with commerce, but she sensed immediately the three men had had dealings in the past and liked each other.

To her surprise the conversation, although heated at times, was not without humour, and in spite of it being two against one Lucas more than held his own and manipulated events skilfully and quietly until he had obtained most of what he had been after.

That this wasn't lost on Jim Clarkson became evident as the four made their goodbyes in the car park. 'He's a wily operator, your Mr Kane,' Jim told her as he shook her hand in farewell. 'But of course you know that.'

'That was exactly what he said about you, Mr Clarkson.' Kim dimpled at the grey-haired, elderly man as she spoke and he laughed out loud, his blue eyes frankly appreciative of the beautiful woman in front of him.

'Flattery will get you everywhere, my dear.'

Lucas had been standing to one side, surveying them from eyes that reflected the winter sky overhead, and now he moved forward, cupping Kim's elbow as he said, 'I'll phone you tomorrow, Jim, once my accountant has looked into a couple of matters.'

'Goodbye, Mrs Allen.' Robert Clarkson had put out his hand as he spoke, forcing Lucas to delay his departure. 'It was nice meeting you,' he said softly, his eyes warm.

'Likewise.'

Robert opened his mouth to say more but Kim found herself whisked across the car park, which had been swept clean of even the faintest trace of snow, before the younger man could speak and then she was in the Aston Martin with the door firmly shut.

That had bordered on rudeness. She watched her boss walk round the bonnet of the car but could read nothing from the bland expression on the craggy face. But perhaps he was in a hurry to return to the office for some reason?

'That went well.'

They had just drawn out of the car park and she had acknowledged Robert's wave—the younger Clarkson standing by a superb dark-blue Mercedes—with a smile and an inclination of her head before she turned to answer Lucas. In spite of the positive content of his words, the tone had suggested something different.

'Yes, I thought so,' she agreed politely.

'You seemed to hit it off well with the Clarksons,' Lucas said expressionlessly.

'You were right—they're nice people.'

Lucas nodded sagely but made no comment.

Kim stared at the cool hard profile for a moment longer, feeling there was something here she had missed, but at a loss to know exactly what.

It was the same when they got back to the offices. Lucas disappeared into his after some curt instructions regarding the notes she had taken during lunch, but he seemed distracted somehow—irritated, even.

Kim found she didn't care. The roller-coaster of emotions she had been riding all day had taken its toll and she was physically and mentally exhausted, needing every scrap of concentration she had left to transcribe her notes into neatly printed pages. The excellent lunch didn't help the feeling of tiredness either; for the first time since she didn't know when she would have loved an afternoon nap, her stomach replete and her brain frazzled.

At half-past four she took a pile of paperwork into Lucas and placed it on his desk.

'Thank you.' He didn't look up.

'I'll come back in ten minutes when you've had a chance to sign the letters; they're on the top,' Kim said evenly.

'Fine.' His voice was distracted and he still didn't raise his head.

She was halfway to the door when she remembered she hadn't mentioned a report the financial director's secretary had just delivered and which she'd placed in the pile, and she turned swiftly, the words on her lips, only to have them freeze as she found him watching her.

Their eyes met and held for an eternity, glittering silver on dark brown, and then his gaze wandered to a tendril of hair which had escaped the neat braid at the back of her head. 'Your colouring is very unusual,' he said almost absently. 'Blonde hair with such dark eyes.'

'My hair is natural.' It was a touch defensive.

'I know; I can tell,' he said softly.

Of course he would be able to tell, with all the blondes—natural and otherwise—he must have known in his time. The fact that her mind had registered the thought, rather than the thought itself, disturbed Kim, and to cover her confusion she found herself babbling, 'Melody has the same blonde hair and dark eyes, actually.'

He nodded slowly. 'Genetic. Perhaps one of your parents had the same colouring?' His voice was very deep and very soft.

Kim wanted to gulp, her throat seemed to be closing up, but she breathed out through her nose and said calmly, 'My mother. I don't remember her but I have a photograph. My father was blonde too but he had blue eyes.'

'Right.'

He hadn't moved a muscle and there was no need to feel threatened but that was exactly what she did feel. Get a hold of yourself, she warned herself silently. This is a perfectly respectable conversation and you're acting like an idiot.

'I…I'll come back in a few minutes for the letters, then.'

'What?' Her ruthlessly focused, coldly intelligent boss stared at her vacantly for a moment and then nodded abruptly. 'Yes, do that, Kim.'

He lowered his head and she was off the hook, but it wasn't until she was in her own office again that Kim realised she hadn't told him about the financial report he had been waiting for. Well, she wasn't going in there again—he'd find it, she told herself shakily.

It was another ten minutes before he buzzed her, and as she took the papers he held out to her her eyes sprang to meet his as Lucas said quietly, 'Sit down a moment, Kim. There's something I need to say to you.'

What now? She sat demurely on the edge of the chair in front of the desk, her knees tightly together and her expression reserved.

'As my secretary you are privy to all sorts of confidential information that the rest of my employees are not.'

Lucas's voice was even and steady and Kim wasn't sure if he required an answer to what had seemed like a statement, but she said, 'Yes, of course.'

'You will find that people try to get to me through you for various reasons, some important and some not so important. There will also be instances when you will be approached on a personal level, but June found it was more circumspect to keep herself to herself at work and reserve her friendships for those individuals unconnected with Kane Electrical.'

What was he getting at? 'But I thought her future husband was a supplier for Kane Electrical?' Kim asked in surprise.

Granite eyes flickered briefly. 'The exception that proved the rule,' Lucas said crisply.

Right. Kim stared at him bewilderedly. Was that all?

'The thing is, Kim...' Lucas paused, his eyes tight on hers, and as she had many times before Kim felt as though his mind was looking straight into hers, probing, dissecting her secret thoughts and fears.

'Yes?' So what was the thing?

'I think you might be having a telephone call from Robert Clarkson,' Lucas said coolly.

'Robert Clarkson?' Kim stared at him as if he was mad. 'Why would Robert Clarkson call me?'

'Isn't it obvious?' His voice was harsher and he must have realised this because it was back to its normal even tone when he said, 'He likes you. When you were in the ladies' cloakroom at lunch he was asking about you.'

Kim was totally taken aback and her honest bewilderment was written all over her face. 'But...but I didn't... I mean...'

'You didn't notice.' It was a statement and spoken with mild exasperation.

'No, I didn't.' Kim sensed criticism and her hackles rose accordingly. 'I was there in the capacity of your secretary and doing a job, that's all.' And who would notice another man with Lucas Kane in the vicinity? The dangerousness of the thought shocked her and brought a flood of hot colour into her face.

'Very commendable.' It was dry and did nothing to soothe her ruffled feathers. 'Well, take it from me, Robert will contact you in the near future and suggest lunch or dinner—a date, anyway. Of course with Kane Electrical and Clarkson International being involved in delicate negotiations at the moment...'

'You think he would try and use me to gain an advantage?' she asked stiffly. More to the point, he thought she would be stupid enough to discuss confidential matters with every Tom, Dick and Harry! How dared he? How *dared* he treat her as though she had so little sense or respect for her position that she would allow herself to be so indiscreet?

'Not necessarily.'

'Then what?' Her voice had risen but she couldn't help it. She was so *mad*.

'I was merely pointing out certain factors, that's all.' His eyes were hard chips of narrowed ice now but Kim was too incensed to take heed.

'I work for you, and you have the right to demand my absolute loyalty and discretion with all matters connected to that work, but you do not have the right to tell me who

I can and can't date outside of these four walls,' Kim bit out tightly, her face chalk-white except for two red patches of colour on her cheekbones.

She had no intention of dating Robert Clarkson—she had no intention of dating anyone ever again—but if Lucas Kane thought he owned her, body and soul, he had another think coming. The arrogance—the sheer unadulterated *arrogance* of the man!

'Neither would I try,' he grated angrily.

'Oh, come on, that's exactly what you've just tried,' she flung back furiously.

There was an electric silence which vibrated the airwaves but for all his inward rage Lucas Kane's face was as unrevealing as a bare canvas. He had sat there all through that damned lunch and watched Rob fall over himself to impress her; it had been pathetic, he told himself savagely. And she'd smiled back at Rob in a way she had never looked at him; she hadn't flinched when Rob had touched her arm or helped her on with her coat, damn it.

He had battled with his feelings all afternoon, feelings new to him and acutely disturbing. He'd always prided himself on being a logical man first and foremost, a man who kept his life free and uncluttered and who liked his relationships to follow suit.

Human triangles, sentiment, jealousy—he had always found such matters irritating and non-productive and avoided them like the plague. He liked women who thought like men in the emotional sense—or like him, at least. Non-clinging, independent, able to let go when the affair ended with no tears and no messy entanglements.

And he still thought like that, damn it. Nothing had changed. *Nothing.*

'There's no need for hysterics.' His voice was as cold as ice and his arctic eyes drilled into her like unrelenting steel. 'I was simply putting you on your guard, that's all. You have worked for me for three months and nothing of this nature has cropped up before.'

He rose as he finished speaking, walking across to the door and opening it as he said, 'Perhaps you would make sure those letters are in the post tonight.'

He was dismissing her. Like a headmaster with an errant child! Kim rose to her feet, her clenched fists crumpling the papers in her grasp and forcing her to relax her fingers slightly.

She had intended to sail past him with haughty indifference, her head held high, but the anger that still had her in its grip made her careless. Whether it was the thin heel of her court shoes catching in the carpet or the fact that her legs were shaking so badly, she didn't know, but to her horror she found herself in danger of sprawling at his feet as she felt herself begin to fall just as she reached the doorway.

The letters flew out of her fingers in a whirling arc as she grappled vainly at thin air in an effort to right herself, and then strong arms caught her and brought her thudding against a muscled male chest.

Kim was so dazed and disorientated that she made no sort of move to free herself, and Lucas seemed to have frozen. And then he moved her an inch or so away in order to look down into her face. 'Have you hurt yourself?' His voice was deep and edged with huskiness.

Hurt herself? She didn't know what she had done, held in his arms like this. She could have a broken leg and it wouldn't register.

She knew she had to say something—she couldn't continue staring up into his dark face—but all the half-remembered, forbidden dreams that had haunted her sleep for the last months had come together and it was surreal.

Her hands had landed against the broad wall of his chest and she could feel the thud, thud of his heart beneath her fingertips, the smooth blue silk of his shirt not quite disguising the roughness of body hair beneath it.

Her own heart was pounding, racing the blood through her veins and echoing its thunder in her throat so that it stifled any words she needed to speak to finish this thing quickly and without further embarrassment. She was aware of his harnessed strength, of the power in the bunched muscles of his arms and the magnificent ribcage beneath her palms, but instead of driving her to jerk away—as it should have done—it increased the strange inability to move.

'Kim?' It was a soft murmur, almost a whisper, and then he bent his dark head and nuzzled the golden silk of her hair as he moved her into him again, his voice restrained as he said, 'It's all right; you're okay.'

He had known she was expecting him to kiss her, wanting him to kiss her. And he hadn't.

It was like a deluge of cold water and she pulled free in the next moment, utterly mortified as she bent and quickly gathered up the scattered papers, snapping—when Lucas made a move to help—'I can manage perfectly well, thank you.'

He froze immediately, his voice quiet but with a distinct edge to it when he said, 'Of course you can.'

She had never, not even when Graham had been at his worst, felt such burning humiliation as she was feeling now. The papers retrieved, Kim rose jerkily to her feet, her face flushed and her eyes brilliant with the shame that was making her rigid.

'I'll see that these go off tonight,' she muttered painfully, without looking at Lucas.

He had moved slightly away from the door and now she walked through it quickly, hearing it close behind her with a further stiffening of her already taut limbs.

All she wanted to do was to escape.

Kim stuffed the letters into their envelopes with a feverish haste that took no account of precise folding or anything else. Then, rather than following normal procedure and ringing through to Accounts to inform the junior there that Mr Kane's post was ready for collection, she took it down herself, lingering for a few moments to talk to the financial director's secretary before she returned to the top floor, although afterwards she had no recollection of what they had talked about.

Lucas was speaking on his private line when she walked into her office and she fairly flew round, collecting her coat and turning off the word processor, checking everything was in order, and then scurrying out to the lift as though the devil himself was at her heels.

She had never gone without saying goodnight before—neither had she left before five o'clock, and it was still only five to—but none of that mattered. If she had to face Lucas tonight, look into those mocking silver eyes and see the knowledge of her own weakness in his face, she would crumple. She knew it.

And it wasn't until she was safely in the blue BMW driving away from Kane Electrical that she allowed the first hot tears to fall.

CHAPTER FOUR

AFTER a riotous snowman-building exercise with Melody, followed by hot soup and crumpets smothered with butter and jam, Kim felt a little better.

Okay, so she had made the mother and father of a fool of herself, she admitted silently as she stood washing up the tea things, having sent Melody to tidy her room before her nightly bath. She had stood there like someone who had lost their wits staring up into his face, but perhaps he hadn't known what she was thinking? *She* hadn't realised what she was thinking until he *hadn't* kissed her.

She gave a small smothered sigh and gazed unseeingly over the back garden, the large snowman she and Melody had made gazing back at her unblinkingly from his vantage point in the middle of the lawn.

The crazy thing was she didn't want Lucas to kiss her, not in the cold light of day. It was the last thing she wanted, she told herself firmly. Even if Lucas Kane hadn't been her boss, she wouldn't have contemplated getting involved with him in a million years, or any man for that matter. But especially Lucas Kane.

He was too dominant a man, too strong physically and mentally and much too ruthless and cold and cynical. And too charismatic, too darkly sensual and magnetic, the little voice in her head jeered bluntly, prompted by her conscience and innate honesty.

'Oh, whatever!' She swished her hands irritably in the hot soapy water, angry with herself and Lucas Kane and the whole world. She didn't recognise herself any more; that was most of the problem. Or perhaps didn't trust herself was a better definition? He had made no move towards her—in fact, he had shown only too clearly that afternoon that she held as much attraction for him as a piece of wet lettuce—so she had to accept the problem was all hers. And it wasn't a problem, it really wasn't—not unless she made it one.

That reasoning helped, a little.

For some reason Lucas Kane affected her like no other man she had known. She had thought she was sexually attracted to Graham, but now she knew she hadn't even understood the first thing about such an emotion.

So... Her hands became still again and her eyes dark and unfocused. She either faced facts, got a hold on her ridiculous hormones and made sure an incident like this afternoon never happened again, or she left. It was as simple as that at root level. And if she left it was goodbye wonderful salary, goodbye car and very probably goodbye this house, because she wasn't at all sure she would ever get another job like her present one. Could she really justify robbing Melody of what promised to be a glowing future, simply because she found her boss the most sexy thing since Adam first walked the earth? No, she couldn't.

Her hands automatically found a teaplate and washed it.

She had to go into work tomorrow as though nothing had happened. She had worked for him for three months and she could continue to do so; it was mind over matter. And she wouldn't think about how she had told him one minute that she didn't like physical contact, and the next had been all over him. She groaned softly and then took herself to task again. No, keep it drama-free, Kim, she told herself tightly. You weren't all over him, you were just...willing. Oh, hell.

The ringing of the doorbell was a welcome relief to her thoughts, but Kim's brow wrinkled as she went to answer the door. It could only be Maggie, but her friend rarely came unannounced. Perhaps she had had a row with Pete again? Things seemed to be going from bad to worse in that direction and she knew Maggie was getting to the end of her tether with Pete's inability to make any real commitment. Men! Kim was frowning as she opened the door. They were nothing but trouble, the lot of them.

The source of her present and very real trouble was standing straight in front of her, and for a moment Kim could only stare up into Lucas's dark face as she did an imitation of a goldfish in a bowl, her mouth opening and then shutting without emitting a sound.

'I'm sorry to come to your home like this but I've been trying to call you since just before six,' Lucas said coolly. 'I understand that a combination of freezing fog and then this latest snow has brought some telephone lines down.'

'Oh.' Kim stared at him vacantly. The phone hadn't rung since she had been home, but then it rarely did.

'Can I come in?' Lucas asked patiently.

'What?' And then she caught herself, flushing hotly as she said, 'Oh, yes, of course. Come in.'

He looked incredibly big and dark in her little cream-painted hall, and as she indicated for him to walk through into the sitting room she kept a good three feet between them, moving hurriedly to the other side of the room away from his disturbing presence as soon as she could.

He was wearing a thick dark-charcoal overcoat over his suit and it increased the impression of brooding masculinity tenfold, freezing her thought process and making her all of a dither as she said, 'Sit...sit down, won't you?'

'Thanks.' He undid his overcoat before taking the seat she had offered with a wave of her hand, placing both hands on the arms of the easy chair and crossing one knee in a pose that was utter male.

She had thought she would at least have another fourteen hours or so before she had to face him again, and with the memory of the afternoon burning hotly and making her heart pound like a sledge-hammer further small talk was quite beyond Kim. Why was he here?

And then Lucas answered the unspoken question as he said coolly, his voice expressionless, 'I was looking for the financial report Clare sent through today. I'd attached a note to it asking you to confirm a couple of figures but I assume you left that for tomorrow? I couldn't find it when I looked on your desk, though, and I need it to work on tonight along with the Clarkson file.'

'Financial report?' Kim stared at him. 'It was in the papers I gave you this afternoon,' she said uncomprehendingly.

'I know.' His voice was still flat. 'I looked at it and made the notes and gave it back to you along with the correspondence to go out tonight,' he repeated evenly.

She continued to stare at him but now a terrible suspicion had rendered her dumb.

The silver eyes hadn't changed expression, neither had he spoken again, but somehow—in spite of Lucas's apparent calmness and immobility—Kim knew the same suspicion had occurred to him.

'You're sure you gave it back to me?' she asked faintly.

He nodded once.

'And…and you can't find it?'

He shook his head.

She felt sick, her stomach churning so much it threatened to let go of the soup and crumpets. 'I…I didn't see it,' she admitted miserably.

'Which means?'

The full enormity of the colossal mistake was sweeping over her. She hadn't been thinking straight when she had stuffed the letters into their envelopes that afternoon; she could easily have included the report with one of them. That was bad enough in itself, but it was a highly confi-

dential breakdown of profit margins and sources to several
suppliers, one or two of which Lucas had written to that
day. If the report was in one of those envelopes...

Kim didn't prevaricate, taking a deep breath which didn't
ease her thumping heart at all before she said, 'I must have
sent it out with the letters. I'm terribly sorry, Lucas.'

'Any idea which one?' He hadn't raised his voice by so
much as a decibel.

She wanted to shut her eyes and wring her hands, at the
very least to groan out loud, but she shook her head, her
eyes tragic as she said again, 'I'm so sorry, I really am.
There's no excuse for such carelessness. I'll resign immediately, of course.'

'I don't want you to resign, Kim. I want you to think
and tell me which letter the damn report is in.'

'I don't *know*.' It was in the form of a wail. 'It could be
in any one of them.'

'Including Turners and Breedon?' In spite of all his efforts Lucas's voice was no longer expressionless.

'Yes.'

He looked down at his handmade shoes, the blue-black
of his thick short hair adding to the overall dark maleness
which seemed so alien in her little home, and Kim watched
him helplessly. How could she have been so irresponsible,
so criminally slipshod? This was the end; it had to be. Even
if he didn't demand her resignation right away there was
no chance of him ever trusting her again.

Useless to tell herself that she had been suffering the
worst attack of panic she'd ever experienced in her life at
the time of the blunder. That the feel of being in his arms,
even for a few short moments, had caused emotions she'd
never thought to feel again—never *had* felt, really, because
certainly Graham, even in their carefree university days,
hadn't inspired such overwhelming sexual awareness.

Lucas Kane didn't want to hear all that, even if she could

tell him—which of course was impossible. She would rather be hung, drawn and quartered!

'Mummy?'

As Kim's eyes focused on the tiny figure of her daughter standing in the doorway she was aware of Lucas's head snapping upwards, but she was already walking across the room, her voice soft as she said, 'It's all right, sweetheart. You finish clearing up your room and I'll be up in a minute.'

'I have finished.' Melody had sensed some kind of atmosphere and wasn't about to be ushered away without protest. 'Hello.' She cut through anything Kim might have said with the directness of childhood as she stared straight into the silver-grey eyes and added, 'I'm Melody Allen.'

'How do you do, Melody? I'm Lucas Kane,' Lucas said softly.

'My mummy works for you,' Melody said interestedly.

'That's right, darling.' It was Kim who answered and now her voice held a note Melody recognised when she added, 'Go and start getting ready for your bath *now*.' For some reason, and Kim couldn't have explained it even to herself, she didn't want her daughter to have anything to do with this man. Not even in the slightest way.

Melody nodded and even took one step backwards into the hall, but her innate friendliness added to healthy curiosity was too much, and her little voice piped up, again directed at Lucas when she said, 'We made a snowman and had crumpets for tea. Have you seen my snowman?'

'Not yet but I'd like to,' Lucas said quietly, smiling across at the small child who was a charming miniature of her beautiful mother. 'Perhaps you can show him to me after your bath?'

This was getting out of hand. 'I don't allow Melody to bathe herself,' Kim put in quickly, wishing he would go. The letters had gone and there was nothing she could do tonight to retrieve the situation. She would resign—eat humble pie, grovel, whatever he demanded—tomorrow, but she couldn't cope with seeing him in her home or talking to her daughter. It made him too…human.

'I can wait.' The silvery eyes challenged her to say more and Kim knew, she *knew* he had read her mind again.

'But you must be very busy—'

'I can wait,' he repeated smoothly.

'Do you like crumpets?' Melody had clearly decided this silly adult conversation had gone on long enough. 'We've got some left and you can have one if you like,' she offered magnanimously.

Lucas raised his gaze from Melody's sweet, dark-eyed face to her mother's horrified one, and Kim noticed his mouth was twitching and the silver eyes were bright with barely concealed amusement. 'I love crumpets,' he said very seriously, lowering his gaze to Melody's, 'and as I haven't had my tea yet that sounds great.'

'Great' wasn't quite the word she would have chosen. Kim stared helplessly, first at Melody and then at Lucas, who was returning her daughter's grin, and knew she had been outmanoeuvred by a pair of experts.

'You haven't eaten?' she murmured weakly.

'No, Kim, I haven't eaten,' he agreed quizzically.

She didn't believe this! How on earth had she found herself in this situation? she asked herself with silent despair. 'We…we had hot soup and rolls followed by crumpets with butter and jam,' she managed fairly distinctly, despite the choking feeling in her throat, 'but I can rustle up an omelette or a pizza if you'd prefer?'

'Soup and crumpets sound good to me.' He was speaking to her but smiling at Melody as he spoke, and again the panicky sensation took Kim's breath away.

It made sense to fix Lucas's meal before she took Melody up for her bath, but she didn't want to leave her daughter with her boss. She didn't want them to get on too well—for Melody to like him. Her brain was racing but the small-mindedness of her thoughts wasn't lost on Kim. But she *needed* to keep him absolutely separate in her head, she told herself frantically, isolated under the heading 'work' and totally detached from her personal life. She didn't dare question why; she just knew it was imperative.

'Do you want to come and help me fix a tray for Mr Kane?'

In spite of the gentleness of her mother's voice, Melody knew a rhetorical question when she heard one, and now the small blonde head nodded obediently.

A larger, dark head across the room registered the message in the 'Mr Kane', but the crystal-clear eyes continued to smile at the little girl as Lucas said softly, 'Thanks, Melody, and I look forward to seeing that snowman later.'

'Make yourself comfortable.' Kim couldn't get out of the room fast enough. 'I'll bring you a coffee in a moment, or perhaps you'd like a glass of wine?'

'I'm driving.' It was an answer in itself and Kim recalled he hadn't had anything stronger than mineral water at lunch, although the wine had been flowing freely and the other two men had imbibed.

A sudden memory—vivid in all its distasteful clarity—of Graham downing half a bottle of vodka before breakfast and then wondering why she had refused to let him take her and Melody to the shops in the car reared its head. It had resulted in a huge row; he had actually struck her that morning.

'Kim?'

Something of her thoughts must have shown on her face because Lucas's voice was sharply concerned, and now Kim realised she had been staring at him without seeing him. She murmured something about having remembered she'd left the gas on and stepped into the hall quickly, shutting the door behind her.

Brilliant. As Melody chattered away while they heated the soup and put the crumpets under the grill, Kim's mind was buzzing. Now not only would he think she was grossly inadequate at work he would think she was lackadaisical at home too. Left the gas on. Kim wrinkled her small straight nose. The cottage was all electric!

She sent Melody upstairs to begin undressing before she took the tray through to the sitting room. Ridiculous, maybe, she acknowledged silently as she turned the handle of the door—nearly upsetting the tray in the process—but the easy way Lucas had with the child had disturbed her. *He* disturbed her, always, but she hadn't expected him to know how to talk to children somehow. She would have thought he'd be even more cold and distant than he was with most adults, but he'd been warm, relaxed, his natural hardness quite gone. And she hadn't liked how it had made her feel.

Lucas had taken off his overcoat and his suit jacket and pulled his tie loose when she walked into the room, and as she glanced at him—sitting in apparent lazy relaxation in front of the flickering coal fire the sitting room boasted—Kim felt a bolt of electricity shoot right down to her toes.

'Nice, the real fire.' His voice was deep, low in his throat, and his eyes were unfathomable.

Kim nodded tensely, watching him straighten himself in the chair with something approaching panic as her gaze seemed to lock on hard male thighs. 'The previous owners had resisted the convenience of an artificial fire, so we followed suit,' she said tightly, her cheeks flushed as she handed him the tray. 'With central heating the cottage gets as warm as toast but a fire is so cosy on winter nights.'

Kim knew she was speaking too quickly, her words falling over themselves, but she was so flustered it was a miracle she could talk at all, she told herself desperately.

She smelt like apples and magnolia flowers and baby powder. Lucas felt his body respond to her closeness, the hungry stirring of hard male arousal, and kept his voice easy and cool when he said, 'This looks wonderful. Thank you.'

'It's the least I can do, in the circumstances.' It wasn't quite what she had intended to say, or rather his response to her innocent words—the faintly lifted sardonic eyebrow and devastatingly wry twist to his undeniably sexy mouth indicated he had put a different interpretation on her ingenuously polite reply—and Kim found herself scurrying out of the room like a frightened mouse.

Well, she'd handled that well! With the door safely closed behind her Kim sank against it in utter frustration and irritation at her inadequacy. This whole scenario was going from bad to worse.

Melody didn't help much, once she was in the bath and Kim was helping her wash her hair. 'I like Lucas.' It was a definite statement. Melody was one for definite statements and rarely changed her mind about anything.

'Mr Kane, sweetheart.' Kim kept her voice casual and very calm. 'You must call him Mr Kane.'

'Why?' A small nose wrinkled bewilderedly.

'Because...because it's polite, with him being Mummy's boss.'

'I like Mr Kane, then.' The little soapy body wriggled round so Melody could stare her straight in the eyes. 'Do you, Mummy? Do you like Mr Kane?'

'Of course I do,' Kim said briskly. 'Now, it's your night for clean pyjamas, young lady. Do you want your teddy bear ones or the ones with little flowers that Aunty Maggie bought you for Christmas?'

The distraction succeeded. It was an important decision and one which needed some consideration.

It was another ten minutes before Kim led Melody—impossibly angelic in forget-me-not-flowered pyjamas and Minnie Mouse slippers—into the sitting room for a cursory goodnight to Lucas. At least, that was what Kim had planned it would be. Lucas and her daughter had different ideas.

'I like your pyjamas.'

It was the first thing Lucas said and nothing could have guaranteed his esteem in Melody's eyes more.

'Aunty Maggie bought them for me.' Great dark eyes locked with silver. 'And Father Christmas brought my slippers. He brought me lots and lots of presents.'

'Lucky old you.' Lucas made a funny face. 'He didn't bring me anything.'

Melody giggled conspiratorially. 'That's because you're a grown-up, silly.'

'Oh, is that what it was? I did wonder.'

Melody giggled some more, moving to stand close to his chair with one tiny hand on his knee. 'You can have one of my chocolates if you like,' she offered solemnly. 'I had a big tin and Mummy only lets me have one every night because she wants me to have no fillings in my teeth.'

'Wise Mummy.'

There were all manner of alarm bells going off in Kim's mind but before she could say anything Lucas had bent down and lifted Melody onto his lap, his voice a stage whisper as he said, 'What I would really like is for you to show me that snowman. Would that be okay with you?'

'Uh-huh.' Melody had wound one arm round his neck, her small face close to his as she whispered back, 'His name is Mr Snow. I named him that.'

'I can't think of a better name.'

She didn't like this. She didn't like this at all. Kim had

combed out her severe office braid and changed into jeans
and a sweatshirt before going into the garden with Melody,
and now she flicked back her heavy fall of hair, her voice
sharp as she said, 'Show Mr Kane the snowman and then
it's bedtime, sweetheart.'

'Lucas.' It was quiet and even but something in his tone
set Kim's heart hammering. 'You can call me Lucas,
Melody.'

'But Mummy said...'

'Yes?' Melody had turned to look across at Kim confusedly. 'What did Mummy say?' Lucas asked softly.

'She said I had to call you Mr Kane because it's polite.'

'And Mummy is right,' Lucas said silkily. 'But now I've
said I want you to call me Lucas it's polite to do that,
okay?'

'Okay.' Melody wriggled happily, clearly captivated, and
Kim silently ground her teeth in impotent rage. Who did
he think he was, muscling in here, talking his way into a
meal and then countermanding her instructions to her
daughter? And then she remembered the reason for his call
and the rage subsided as quickly as it had flared into life.

She had committed an unforgivable mistake and he
would have had every right to storm in here tonight crying
for blood. Instead he had been amazingly calm and reasonable. She didn't know what he was going to say to her once
they were alone, but she couldn't fault his attitude in front
of Melody. So...she owed him a little latitude.

She kept repeating that to herself when he stood to his
feet in the next instant and wrapped Melody in his overcoat
before the three of them paid brief homage to Mr Snow,
Melody's stringy arms tight round Lucas's broad neck, but
she drew the line at Melody's request that Lucas read her
a bedtime story.

'No story tonight, sweetheart.' She took Melody from
Lucas at the bottom of the stairs once they were inside the

cottage again, handing him his coat with a tight smile. 'Mr Kane and I have some important work things to discuss, so you've got to promise Mummy you'll be a good girl and go straight to sleep tonight.'

'Aw...' Melody pouted, peering at Kim from under her eyelashes, but when she saw her mother's face was adamant she gave in with her usual good humour and Kim was downstairs again within two or three minutes.

She paused at the sitting room door before opening it, her stomach turning over, and then smoothed down her sweatshirt and wiped suddenly clammy hands on her jeans. If he was going to shout and scream he would have done so immediately, wouldn't he? But it wasn't just that possibility that was churning her insides and she knew it.

'You have a charming daughter.' Lucas was standing at the window as she entered the room and Kim's heart took a mighty jump as he turned to face her. 'She's a credit to you.'

'Thank you.' Kim stood just inside the door, uncertain of whether to sit or continue standing. This was *her* home, her little castle, but she felt as though she were the guest, she told herself crossly. How did he make her feel like that?

'Can she remember her father at all?'

It wasn't what she had expected him to say and he read the knowledge in the darkening of her velvet brown eyes. Perhaps he shouldn't bring the subject of her husband up again, Lucas acknowledged silently, but he needed to know much more about this reserved, honey-skinned, golden-haired woman and he had a distinct advantage tonight while she was feeling bad about the report. He felt no remorse in thinking this way; in the early days of his joining the family firm his father had taught him always to look for the weak spot in one's opponent and capitalise on it, and he'd found he had a natural aptitude for such ruthlessness.

And Kim was an opponent. He didn't know quite how

it had happened but he knew instinctively it was the case. For some reason she saw him as the enemy and it was grating more and more with every day that passed.

'Her father?' Kim thrust her hands deep into the pockets of her jeans, her face tense. 'No, she can't remember Graham.'

'Come and sit down, Kim.' Lucas indicated the sofa as he walked over to the chair he had vacated earlier, and again it was as if he were the host and she the guest.

She sat down on the very edge of the cushions but as he drew his chair at an angle to the sofa it brought him much too close and so she shifted back in the seat, moving slightly away as she did so. 'I'm very sorry about the report, Lucas.' Her voice was tight and formal. 'If it's in the wrong envelope I know what damage it might do, so the offer stands about my resignation.'

He stared at her for a moment, leaning forward with his elbows on his knees, although he was careful not to touch her. The warm fragrance of her nearness invaded his air space and his senses were registering how much younger she looked with her hair loose about her shoulders, uninhibited even. But looks were deceptive. He could feel the tension in her like a live thing, keeping him at bay.

'I joined Kane Electrical straight from university and I was as green as they come,' Lucas said quietly, his deep, slightly husky voice with its trace of an accent causing her nerve endings to quiver. 'But I was keen.'

He smiled at her, the silver-grey eyes wrinkling at the edges, and Kim forced herself to smile back although it was just a movement of her mouth. He had rolled up his sleeves while she had been out of the room and his muscled forearms were covered in a liberal dusting of black silky hair, and in the position in which he was sitting—with his dark head close to hers and the tanned jawline dark with a day's growth of stubble—it was impossible to ignore his flagrant masculinity.

'My father is a cautious Englishman and my mother a fiery and impetuous Colombian, so I've had to learn to temper my mother's explosive genes and perhaps take more risks on the paternal side. It works...mostly.'

Kim nodded. So that was where the echo of an accent came from. His mother.

'However...' Lucas paused, aware he had her interest. 'In my first year of working for my father, my mother's genes were rampant. I prefer that as an excuse than the foolishness of crass youth. I took a risk, a big risk, off my own back. There was no real need for it, I guess, but perhaps I felt the need to prove myself. I don't know. Anyway, it was a mistake, a huge one; it nearly broke us. It makes your slip-up very meagre in comparison. I never made that mistake again.'

He was looking at her very closely, his eyes intently searching her wide-eyed face. 'You will never make the same mistake again, Kim,' he said very softly, and somehow she got the impression he was talking about more than her blunder with the report.

Kim drew in a deep breath, fighting the sudden and unwelcome tears that were pricking at the back of her eyes. 'It's...it's very good of you to look at it like that,' she managed faintly, keeping strictly to the matter of the day and refusing to acknowledge any hidden connotations in what he was saying. 'But I'm aware it could be very embarrassing for you.'

'I'm not easily embarrassed.' He smiled, an unconsciously sexy quirk to his hard firm mouth, and the breath caught in her throat.

The flickering glow from the fire, the strength and warmth and irresistible drawing power of his dark magnetism were too seductive, too dangerous, and Kim surprised them both when she leapt to her feet, her voice high as she said, 'Coffee. I'll fetch some coffee.'

'Great.' His voice was casual and relaxed as he too stood to his feet, and as he reached out and took her hand his face didn't reveal the anger he felt as she stiffened against his touch. 'Just put it down to experience, Kim,' he said softly. 'Learn from it, take the positive and leave the negative on the side of the plate and don't let it cripple you.'

He *was* talking about more than work.

She hesitated and then raised her head to meet his eyes, her gaze wary. 'That's easier said than done.'

'Possibly.' He could feel her trembling slightly and it checked the crazy impulse he had to pull her into him and devour her mouth; the strength of his desire shocked him. He had never had any trouble in keeping work and play separate, in fact he would go so far as to say he had felt contempt in the past for any business associates who had been foolish enough to mix the two, but this was different. But perhaps that was what they all thought.

The heat from his fingers seemed to be flowing into her, trickling into every nerve and sinew and setting her body alive with a strange electric current. What would it be like to be kissed by a man like Lucas Kane? Kim gave up the fight to dismiss the thought that had been paramount for most of the evening. Thrilling, exciting, out of this world. He'd know how to kiss. Sexual expertise was there in his eyes, his body, even the way he walked and moved...

She jerked her hand free, disguising the gesture with a tight little laugh as she said, 'This won't get the coffee percolating.'

Damn the coffee. Lucas smiled blandly. 'Can I help?'

The thought of him in the close confines of her little kitchen was overwhelming. 'No, it's fine. I won't be a minute.'

Lucas's thick black lashes swept down, hiding his expression from her, and his voice was easy and controlled as he resumed his seat, saying, 'No hurry.'

No hurry? Once in the kitchen Kim leant her hot forehead against the cool impersonal surface of a cupboard and breathed deeply for several seconds. Her fingers were still tingling from his touch and her legs were actually shaking, she realised with a little dart of disbelief. It might be no hurry to him but she wanted him out of her house as soon as possible.

He was dangerous. She moved away from the cupboards and stared out of the window to where the snowman was still standing patiently in his white frozen world, and remembered how Melody had clung to Lucas as he had enthused over their handiwork.

Very, very dangerous. Kim's eyes narrowed and she felt something very cold douse the heat inside her as she switched on the coffee machine.

If Graham hadn't died when he had, she would have left him within weeks, if not days, anyway. The abuse when he was drunk had been becoming increasingly nasty, and the shopping incident had happened the day before his accident. She had known it was the end of the line for their marriage then; she wouldn't risk putting Melody in danger.

She hadn't loved him any more at that stage; she hadn't loved him for months, even though she had stayed because of his threats of what he would do to Melody and to her if she left him.

But that morning when he had struck her had cut the last tentative threads holding her to the marriage. It had happened to be her in the firing line then; it could have been Melody another time and the thought of that was insupportable.

But she hadn't had to leave. Graham had died, and in spite of all his death had uncovered she had felt a strengthening of her spirit, a determination that she would build a good life for her precious child. And a good life meant never putting Melody at risk again, never allowing a third party to come into their world. Friends were different, and Maggie had been wonderful, but a man...

She had made a terrible mistake in her choice of a partner and she couldn't trust it wouldn't happen again.

Melody liked Lucas. And perhaps he was only being friendly and supportive to her about the report incident, but she didn't dare allow the kind of matey relationship to grow between them she wouldn't have necessarily thought twice about with any other colleague.

She'd work her socks off for him, go the extra mile and beyond as far as her work was concerned—she owed him that at least—but she would keep him very firmly at arm's length. It might make things a little awkward at times but she'd have to cross that bridge when it came to it.

She nodded sharply to the golden-haired reflection in the window, lowered the blind abruptly and set about preparing the coffee tray, her mouth set in a grim determined line that wasn't at all like its normal soft self.

CHAPTER FIVE

CONTRARY to the fear which had gripped Kim when she'd watched the Aston Martin drive away that snowy night in January, Lucas didn't ask one personal question or do more than briefly enquire after Melody in the following few weeks, keeping their relationship focused and pleasant.

The report was returned within a couple of days from a somewhat bewildered friend of Lucas's to whom he had written regarding a forthcoming golf tournament, and was the best possible outcome Kim could have wished for.

February passed with more snow, rigid white frosts and a hectic time at the office as the Clarkson contract was finally settled to Lucas's satisfaction. March was a kinder month weather-wise, but by the end of that month Kim found herself wondering if her relationship with her dynamic boss was quite so cool and controlled as she had thought it was.

He had managed to get under her skin somehow, and not just in the sexual sense—that was something she'd accepted she would have to battle with daily; he was just one exceptional man—but in a hundred other, more subtle ways.

Lucas had a wickedly dry sense of humour for a start and he wasn't averse to laughing at himself, which was a revelation to Kim after Graham's self-important, pontifical attitude to life. She found herself laughing umpteen times a day, and often when she least expected it.

He had the habit of scattering numerous little personal facts about himself and his family into even the most businesslike of their days, and by now Kim knew that his parents had retired to a villa in the sun; that the prolific amount of aunts, uncles and cousins on his mother's side made for some crazy family parties when relations would fly the short journey from Colombia to his parents' home in Florida; that like himself his father had been an only child and his English relations were few and far between, and many other details besides.

Kim was aware that Lucas's large country residence situated well beyond the city limits was home to an elderly housekeeper as well as himself. Martha had been with the family since Lucas was a babe in arms, and besides the two human occupants the mansion housed an assortment of feline inhabitants—all belonging to Martha—and two Great Danes which were Lucas's.

This last had caused Kim one of many disturbed nights in relation to her boss.

She hadn't had him down as an animal-lover before he had mentioned his home situation, or the sort of man who could be altruistic to old ladies who hadn't wanted to leave the country of their birth for warmer climes.

The comfortably cold and detached picture of a cool stainless-steel, remotely controlled bachelor pad with all mod cons and the biggest bed money could buy had taken a knock, and when she had made the mistake of revealing her surprise and preconceptions and Lucas had admitted—charmingly—that a few years before she would have been spot-on, it had been scant comfort.

She wanted—*needed*—to keep him in a neatly labelled box in her mind and, annoying man that he was, he seemed determined to break out of it.

Somehow, and she didn't quite know how he had accomplished it, he had managed to paint a picture on her mind that was quite different from the one she wanted to see when she looked at him. If he had met her head-on in direct challenge she would have been able to cope with it and refuse to take on board Lucas the man, rather than Lucas the ruthless tycoon, but he had trickled himself into her psyche with the steady drip-drip of relentless running water.

He was a brilliant and inexorable strategist. She had seen him in action too many times in business now to doubt it, and had marvelled more than once that his adversaries hadn't seemed to be aware of what he was doing, not realising all the time he was applying an equally ruthless policy with her.

But perhaps she was imagining all this? Kim sat for a moment more in the BMW before squaring her shoulders and opening the car door. Whatever, she couldn't let her guard down with Lucas Kane, not for a moment. That, if nothing else in the whole tangled situation, was crystal-clear.

The March day was damp and mild but very blowy, and in spite of the fact that her parking space was only a few yards away from the main doors of Kane Electrical, the wind had tugged several golden tendrils of hair loose from its customary tight knot at the back of her head by the time she entered the building.

Charlie, the caretaker, was standing in a quiet and empty Reception—it being too early for the rest of the staff yet—and addressed her immediately, saying, 'Power cut, I'm afraid, Mrs Allen. All the lights are out and the lifts are down, but they assure me it won't be too long before we're back in operation.'

'Thanks, Charlie. Looks like it'll be Shanks' pony and the stairs, then.' Kim flashed the elderly man a grin before making for the stairs at the back of an unusually dark Reception and running up them lightly, her mind already grappling with the first few things she had to do that day.

She emerged from the fire door into the top floor corridor dimly lit by the emergency lighting, still concentrating on her imminent workload, and straight into the arms of her esteemed boss with enough force to send them both against the far wall.

She was pressed against the length of him, his arms holding her in instinctive protection against his muscled chest, and as she raised a flushed and breathless face to him, her wind-blown hair curling in shiny, silky strands about her pink cheeks, he made no attempt to let her go.

The hushed dark corridor, the utter absence of all sound or movement made the moment surreal, like a vaguely remembered chimerical dream, and it seemed part of the fantasy when his dark head bent and caught her mouth in a deep languorous kiss that went on and on. His lips were moving against hers slowly as he crushed her closer, his hand cupping her head for deeper penetration as he urged her into an increasingly intimate acceptance of his hungry mouth, and it didn't occur to Kim to even struggle.

There was an insistence, a dominant mastery that demanded rather than asked for her consent and there was no way she could refuse. She had lived this moment so many times, tasted it, savoured it in her dreams, and now, in the shadowy alien confines of the silent corridor, fantasy and fact were combining in overwhelming ecstasy.

Heat was surging in the core of her, lighting flickers of fire in every nerve and sinew, and as her lips parted to allow his probing tongue access into the secret places her body curved closer into him, the physical ache becoming sweeter.

He made a small sound of pleasure deep in his throat and Kim answered it with one of her own, faintly bewildered by her desire. She had lost all thought of where she was, her mind and her emotions totally captive to the sensations he was evoking with such consummate ease. This was the sort of kiss she had dreamt about as a young, romantic teenager before life had taught her such things only existed in the land of make-believe, but this was *real*, this was now.

She was kissing him back in the way she had during her sleeping fantasies, without restraint, hungrily searching for she knew not what.

Graham had not been an adventurous or a thoughtful lover and she hadn't slept with anyone before her husband, therefore her sexual experience was limited to Graham's hasty couplings without much finesse. This was gloriously, frighteningly different.

The warmth and the slowly building ache in the core of her femininity, the spasmodic thrills circulating her bloodstream and causing her breath to shudder and gasp against his warm knowing mouth, were something outside her knowledge and desperately seductive. This was pleasure; this was the sort of pleasure she had read about but never imagined was so fiery, so consuming, so frightening. And she wanted more, much more.

Kim wasn't even aware of the sudden brightness of lights against her closed eyelids, but the whirr of the lift did cause her to open dazed eyes, or perhaps it was the fact that Lucas's mouth had left hers.

'The power's back on.' His voice was thick and husky and he still held her against him, his arousal hard against her softness.

She was trembling, she knew she was trembling, and now that his lips had stopped fuelling the fire that had eaten up all her inhibitions and common sense she felt a growing horror at her complete submission to his lovemaking. And bereft. Bereft at the feeling of loss now it had stopped.

'Let...let go of me.' It was a faint whisper but he didn't argue, his eyes a brilliant silver in the hard, ruthless lines of his face.

'That was unintentional, Kim.'

As she jerked back from him, her hands to her hot face,

the words caught at her. Was he saying he regretted it? She stared at him wildly, her eyes deep pools of black velvet in the flushed smoothness of her face. Probably. But then she had more or less offered herself on a plate and few men would resist such an opportunity. What would have happened if the power hadn't come back on when it did?

She clenched her shaking hands into tight fists at her side, noticing, with further shame, that Lucas was perfectly cool and relaxed. And it was her humiliation that made her say, her voice bitter and tight, 'You mean you just felt a sudden urge for a quickie?'

Immediately the ugly words left her lips she wished them back, the crudeness shocking her, but it was too late. She had said them. Out of pain and anguish, but she'd still said them.

And Lucas was furious. She knew it from the dark colour that flared across the hard cheekbones and the muscle working in his jaw, but his voice was at direct variance to his face when he said icily, 'You rate yourself very cheaply if you believe that.'

'I'd say it's you who rates me cheaply,' she hissed back sharply.

'Then you'd be wrong.' The words were like bullets. 'If you were anyone other than who you are I wouldn't have stopped at a kiss, believe me, Kim.'

What did that mean? That he had stopped because he didn't fancy her that much, or because she was his secretary and it would cause too many complications, or what? 'So you expect me to be grateful you didn't force me?' she snapped bitterly.

'I wasn't using any force.' His voice was soft now, soft and mocking, and his eyes dared her to deny what they both knew. 'You were with me every inch of the way from the second our lips touched.'

'I don't think so!' she flung sarcastically.

'I know so.' He paused, the glittering silver eyes like liquid steel as they held hers. 'But when I take you it won't be in a work situation and on the floor of a corridor, Kim. That's a promise.'

She stared at him, utterly taken aback and more frightened than she had ever been in her life. But not of Lucas. Of the feeling deep inside his softly growled words had evoked. She wanted to hate him or at least dislike him but she couldn't. Neither could she pretend that he was just someone she worked for and dismiss him the moment she left the building; he had woven himself too skilfully into her life for that.

'I resign.' She raised her chin defiantly, her back ramrod-straight. 'As of now.'

'Don't be childish,' he said cuttingly, and before she could say anything more he had stepped past her and opened the door onto the stairs, leaving her alone and shaking.

Childish? She stared at the door, nonplussed by the sudden end to what she had considered the most devastating experience of her entire life. *Childish?* How dared he?

She stood for a moment more and then forced her shaking legs to carry her into the office where she made straight for her little cloakroom.

The flushed, bright-eyed girl in the mirror, with the bruised mouth, was not someone she recognised, and she gazed at herself for a full minute before she could persuade her trembling hands to do something about her dishevelment.

Childish. The word had stung and she couldn't get it out of her mind. Possibly because she had to acknowledge, ruefully and only after another five minutes had ticked by in painful self-assessment, that there was more than grain of truth in it.

She had handled it all wrong from the moment his mouth

had touched hers. What she should have done—what any normal, level-headed, experienced woman would have done—was to accept the kiss lightly, move gracefully out of his arms after a moment or two and make some casual comment to defuse what had been—by his own admission—a momentary impulse on Lucas's part.

Instead she had nearly eaten him alive and then accused him of—she didn't like to think what she had accused him of. She gave a little groan, scraping every tendril of hair back so tightly into the knot that her scalp ached.

He must thing she had a screw loose. The mirror told her that she was once again transformed into the neatly tailored, cool and efficient Mrs Allen—on the outside, at least. Perhaps she did have a screw loose, she admitted weakly. In fact she suspected she had whole box of them jangling about with regard to Lucas Kane. Certainly he had the power to turn her into someone she didn't know, someone who was very different from the reserved, cool, careful person she had believed herself to be before she had worked for him.

She was typing away at her word processor, her mind ten per cent on her work and ninety per cent on Lucas's return, when she heard his voice in the corridor outside talking to someone. Her heart jumped up into her throat but she forced her hands to keep up a steady rhythm, even as every sense in her body tuned itself in to the moment when he would walk through the door.

She thought the other voice belonged to Lucas's general manager, who had his office at the other end of the corridor, but she couldn't be sure; most voices had a habit of lowering themselves deferentially in Lucas's presence.

And then the door opened and, although she kept her eyes on her work, she knew he was looking at her.

'Kim?'

She'd half hoped—coward that she was, she conceded

silently—that he would simply carry on as though nothing had happened, but she might have known Lucas wouldn't take the easy way out. She raised reluctant eyes to meet his piercing grey gaze and the butterflies in her stomach did a war dance.

'We have to discuss this properly. You know that.'

It was a statement, not a question, but she answered it as though it had been the latter when she said, her voice as cool and distant as she could make it, 'There's nothing to discuss.'

His compelling light eyes narrowed at the words. 'If you felt disturbed enough to make that ridiculous suggestion about resigning I'd say there's every need,' he said grimly. He perched on the edge of her desk—a habit of his and one which always sent her senses haywire—and continued to survey her unblinkingly.

Why did he have to be so attractive? she asked herself rawly. So incredibly, overwhelmingly attractive? She dared bet that there wasn't a female in the building, in the whole of Cambridge, who wouldn't jump at the chance of having an affair with Lucas Kane.

Was he seeing someone at the moment? The thought was entirely inappropriate in the circumstances but she couldn't help it.

'I've…I've change my mind about that,' she managed at last.

'Of course you have.' It was dismissive, as though the idea had been so ludicrous it wasn't worth mentioning. 'But nevertheless we need to discuss what happened.'

Her cheeks were scarlet again, she could feel them burning, and yet he was as cool and unfeeling as the polished granite his eyes seemed to have been fashioned from. But he hadn't been so unfathomable and cold when he'd been holding her in his arms. The thought made Kim's cheeks even hotter. He had been aroused then, hugely aroused, and it had been *her* body, her lips and mouth and tongue that had made him tremble with desire. She didn't know if she found the thought alarming or comforting but she did find it exciting, and that was more than dangerous enough to cope with.

'Look, Lucas, I'm prepared to look at it as a mistake, one of those things that happen now and again when people of the opposite sex work so closely together as we do,' Kim said with a steadiness she was proud of. 'It didn't mean anything—'

'The hell it didn't.'

It wasn't at all the response she'd expected and cut off all coherent reasoning. 'Wha…what did you say?'

'Kim, I don't know what sort of man you think I am,' Lucas said smoothly, his thick black lashes masking the flicker of anger her words had wrought, 'but when I kissed you it sure as hell meant something to both of us.'

'I didn't mean I didn't enjoy it,' she said quickly, without thinking. She heard him draw in a quick hard breath and realised her *faux pas*. 'I mean…' Her voice trailed away helplessly.

Lucas rescued her with his normal calm composure. 'You've worked for me for five months and I've wanted to see what you tasted like from day one,' he said as coolly as though he was asking her to type a letter. 'Why do you think I haven't dated anyone in all that time?'

'You haven't?' She checked herself quickly. Breathless murmuring was not the way to deal with this.

'And I've been patient,' he continued with silky quietness. More patient than she'd ever know.

'But…'

''Yes?'

'I work for you.'

Lucas ignored every principle he'd ever worked by and

said calmly, 'So? You're unattached and so am I. That's the only important thing, surely?'

Was he stark staring mad? Kim had spent five months fighting off the most devastating feeling of sexual attraction, which had frightened her far more than it thrilled her—at least, the potential power it gave to Lucas frightened her—and the only reason she was still working for Lucas Kane was because she had convinced herself the attraction was all on her side. To get involved, to have a *relationship* with a man like him, was too alarming, too utterly insane and impossible even to consider.

She stared at him, the breadth of his shoulders under the white silk shirt he was wearing suddenly oppressive, and wetted her dry lips. His eyes followed her tongue unblinkingly, his firm, cynical mouth slightly pursed, and her traitorous libido wanted to explode. It was further confirmation that an affair with Lucas was unthinkable. If he would affect her so badly without even touching her...

'It's out of the question, Lucas.'

'I don't accept that,' he said immediately in answer to her trembling voice. 'I'm not asking you to leap into bed with me—' Liar! his conscience screamed silently '—just for us to get to know each other without the pressure of a work environment.'

'I...I can't do that. There's Melody—'

'Melody isn't a problem.'

'It isn't just that.' She took a deep breath, her mind suddenly clear. 'I don't want to get involved with anyone, a man, ever again,' she stated firmly. 'I've been through all that and it didn't work.'

'With your husband, you mean?' he asked softly. And at her nod he shook his own head, his voice low and husky as he said, 'Don't let him spoil the rest of your life, Kim.'

'I'm not, but it *is* my life now and that's what I like.' Her dark-brown eyes held Lucas's gaze with an earnestness that was almost childlike. 'I...I don't think I'm the sort of person who should ever be with someone else, not really.' Graham had flung that at her once in a drunken rage but the barb had held and dug itself deep into her mind.

'What rubbish.' Kim lifted her chin in unconscious defiance and he added, 'Who told you that? Slimeball?'

'Slime... Oh, Graham?'

He could tell by the flush that rose in her cheeks he was on the right tack and anger thickened his voice as he said, 'Don't judge the whole male race by the lowest specimen, Kim, and sure as hell don't take on board anything he said. The guy was crazy not to appreciate what he had.'

'You don't know how it was,' she said defensively. 'It wasn't just Graham, it was... Oh, you don't know.'

Lucas expelled a silent breath. This was the first time she had talked to him, really talked to him, and he didn't want her to close up again. 'No, I don't know how it was,' he agreed quietly, 'so why don't you tell me?'

'I can't.' The colour had drained from her face, leaving it chalk-white. How could she make someone like Lucas understand what it had been like all those years in the children's home? Wanting, *aching* to belong to a family, to have people she could call her own? And then, as she had gone into her teens and realised it wasn't going to happen, she had purposely grown a protective shell, telling herself she didn't care, that she would make it on her own and blow the rest of the world.

And then Graham had happened in her first year at university. Handsome, charming Graham, sweeping her off her feet with all his attention. She had thought he loved her, believed everything he'd said, and it hadn't been until after they had been married that she had come to realise— through something he had yelled at her in one of their rows—that the main reason he had been interested in her was because several of his friends had wanted her. Graham always had to be the one who was admired and envied.

But Graham had given her Melody. By accident, admittedly, but Melody was worth a hundred times the heartache Graham had put her through. And now she had her family and she didn't need anyone else. She wouldn't let herself need anyone else. Needing Graham had made her vulnerable and exposed and weak and she would never give that power to a man again.

Lucas had watched the changing emotions wash over her white, fragile face and he knew she wasn't about to say any more—not here and now, anyway. She didn't trust him, he wasn't even sure if she liked him very much, but she couldn't deny the physical attraction between them. His bruised ego seized on the thought but it was scant comfort.

No woman had ever treated him as Kim had done. He had thought, at first, that the air of cool restraint would mellow as she settled into the job, but it had got stronger, if anything. That night at her home he had felt as though he was treading on eggshells, damn it, and all the ground he thought he'd gained over the last weeks now seemed to exist only in his imagination. She might look fragile and breakable but she was as hard as iron underneath.

So why didn't he cut his losses and congratulate himself on having an efficient and beautiful secretary who was clearly interested in her career and nothing else, and leave it at that? He had any number of women he could call who had made it clear in the past that they were available. Successful, confident, attractive career women. Women with no hang-ups, no inhibitions.

A loud knock at Kim's outer door, followed by the big, rotund figure of John Powell, Lucas's general manager, effectively finished the conversation. It brought Lucas to his feet; the other man was waving a file at his managing director as he said, 'Those subcontractors you wanted the low-down on? You were right, Lucas. We shouldn't touch them with a barge-pole.'

Perfect timing as always, John. Lucas kept his thoughts to himself, but his voice was curt when he said, 'Come into my office, John, and tell me what you've got.' He didn't alter the tone as he added, 'Coffee when you're ready, Mrs Allen.'

Coffee when you're ready, Mrs Allen.

Kim sat for some moments without moving after the door to Lucas's office had closed and she was alone.

The kiss, their conversation, all the emotion of the last half an hour or so hadn't meant a thing to him, not really. He looked on her as a challenge, if anything—that was it at base level. She hadn't fallen into his arms as women were prone to do with Lucas—she ignored the fact that that was exactly what she had done, both physically and metaphorically, that morning—or fluttered her eyelashes or given him the come-on over the coffee cups.

She rose slowly, angry with herself and Lucas. Did she believe he hadn't dated since she'd started at Kane Electrical? Kim considered the thought as she prepared the coffee tray, her slender hands moving mechanically as she frowned into space. Yes, she thought she did; Lucas wouldn't lie.

Lucas wouldn't lie? The moment it entered her mind, she attacked the thought like a terrier with a rabbit. Just because her boss was honest—brutally honest, on occasion—with regard to his business dealings, it certainly didn't mean he was equally honourable and veracious in his dealings with women, she told herself caustically.

Kim suddenly remembered Graham. She had believed him, trusted him, and look where it had got her. One mistake was understandable; a second would verge on stupidity. And she was not a stupid woman. He had called her that many times. She shut her eyes and could almost hear the echo of past fights. Graham had been cruel, spectacularly cruel when he'd been under the influence of alcohol. She had heard it said that an excess of alcohol revealed the real person beneath the social niceties civilisation imposed on the human race, and in Graham's case it hadn't been pleasant.

By the time she carried in the coffee tray Kim was the epitome of the cool blonde, her mouth set in a polite smile and her manner courteous.

'Thank you.' Lucas raised his dark head and looked straight into her eyes as she placed the tray on his desk, and in spite of her acute discomfort Kim felt there was some genuine concern as his narrowed eyes searched her face.

She berated herself for the weakness as soon as she was safely back in her office. June had said he was a Lothario, hadn't she? Well, Lucas's previous secretary hadn't actually said that *exactly*, she admitted in the next instant, but June had implied that Lucas was a love 'em and leave 'em type, and she ignored that at her peril.

She sipped her own coffee, her head whirling, and then contemplated the pile of work needing her attention with a rueful twist to her lips. Enough. She was here to do a job of work and that was exactly what she would do. This morning had been a regrettable hiccup but that was all it had been. She had to get a handle on this.

Lucas Kane was her boss *and that was all he was*. She would be doubly careful not to infringe on his privacy in any way from this day forth—although she didn't think she had done so before—in order not to give him the wrong impression.

And the things he had said? The little voice in her head was determined to be heard. About wanting to kiss her from day one? Wanting to get to know her better?

Kim breathed in and then out very slowly, flexing her

fingers on the keyboard and refusing to let the feeling of panic consume her. She wouldn't think about it. It might be the easy way out but it was necessary for her sanity!

She had made it perfectly clear to Lucas how she felt about any sort of personal relationship with him. And he was a proud man, arrogant even, and certainly egotistical. He would disregard all that had happened today, if she knew anything about it, pretend it hadn't happened and perhaps even concentrate his attention on some delectable female he could parade in front of her to make the point, that she—his secretary—was easily forgotten. Yes, that was what he'd do.

John Powell left Lucas's office ten minutes later and after a minute or two Lucas popped his head round the interconnecting door. 'I've reserved a table for two at a nice little place I know tonight,' he said expressionlessly. 'Be ready at eight.' And the door closed without further discussion.

CHAPTER SIX

RIGHT up until the moment Kim found herself on Maggie's doorstep, asking her friend if she could call round later to babysit, Kim would have sworn she had no intention of keeping her date with Lucas.

She had told him so several times throughout the course of what had been, for Kim, a particularly trying day, but it had been like talking to a brick wall. And she just didn't know how to deal with such intractability, Kim admitted silently to herself on the drive home from Maggie's.

In the two years since Graham had died she had had to freeze several advances from hopeful suitors, but it had been easy. A polite thank you but no thank you, a severe look if they'd needed further persuasion and that had been that. But what had worked admirably with the manager at the local supermarket, an old university friend of Graham's and one or two hopeful admirers from clients of Curtis & Brackley had not cut any ice with Lucas Kane.

She had tried to keep everything on a strictly businesslike basis that day, but Lucas had appeared to find her efforts amusing rather than anything else, Kim reflected irritably as she fixed Melody's tea.

But she would spell it out for him tonight, in letters a mile high if necessary, she told herself grimly. She was *not* going to start a relationship with anyone in the forseeable future, least of all Lucas Kane. Her priority in life was Melody—first and foremost. She didn't want or need anyone else.

Maggie arrived early but Kim had known she would. She hadn't been able to say anything more than that she needed

101

her friend to babysit for eight o'clock when she had called by on her way home from collecting Melody, conscious of small ears twitching, but when Maggie had asked—naturally enough—where Kim was going and with whom, and she had mentioned Lucas Kane, Maggie's eyes had nearly popped out of her head.

Melody was tucked up in bed waiting for Maggie to arrive and read her a story, and after Maggie had called up to say she wouldn't be a minute or two, she had taken Kim's arm in a powerful grip and whisked her into the little sitting room.

'Well?' Maggie's nice homely face was agog. 'What gives with the tycoon?'

'Lucas, you mean?'

'You have more than one fabulously rich and gorgeous man asking you out?'

'He's not gorgeous.' It was too quick and they both knew it, and as Kim watched Maggie's eyes narrow speculatively she said more carefully, 'I mean he's just my boss, that's all.'

'And he's taking you out to dinner as what? A little treat for one of his employees?' Maggie asked a trifle sarcastically. 'Come on, Kim, this is Maggie, remember? So, I ask you again, what gives?'

'Oh, Maggie.' It was a hushed wail. 'It's all such a *mess*.' She told Maggie all of it and at the end Maggie nodded sagely, like a wise little ginger owl.

'I knew you'd been on edge these last months but I thought it was just worry about holding down the job,' she said quietly, her eyes sympathetic. 'Why didn't you tell me before, Kim? It might have helped. I don't pretend to have all the answers—look at me and Pete—but I'm always ready to listen.'

'I know.' Kim lifted tragic eyes. 'And perhaps I'm being ridiculous at panicking anyway. I'm only going out for dinner with him and any other girl would be only too pleased at the opportunity of an evening with Lucas Kane.'

'You're not any other girl, though,' Maggie said gently, 'and perhaps he has the good sense to realise it. Maybe he's serious about you, Kim.'

'I hope not.' Kim's voice was suddenly firmer. 'It's a terrific job and I'd hate to have to leave it.'

'You'd do that? Even fancying him the way you do?'

Kim dragged in a deep breath and expelled it quietly. 'I don't want a man in my life, Maggie,' she said grimly. 'Not now, not ever. I've done all that, I've got the T-shirt, and in my case it really is once bitten, twice shy.'

'But he wouldn't be like Graham,' Maggie said softly. 'You do see that, don't you? You can't let Graham ruin your life, Kim.'

'Funny, that's exactly what Lucas said.' Kim smiled at Maggie, a sad little bitter smile as she added, 'But I don't see it that way. Besides, how long do you think a man like Lucas would be interested in someone like me? A month— two, maybe? It might stretch to six at a pinch. I don't belong in his world, Maggie.'

'How do you know that unless you give it a try?' Maggie asked reasonably.

'I know, all right.' Kim suddenly wanted the conversation to end. 'Anyway, there's Melody to consider too, don't forget. I don't want her getting fond of someone only for them to disappear in a little while. There's one or two of her friends who have ''uncles'' who are here today and gone tomorrow, a new father-figure every time the wind changes. My child isn't going to have to go through that.'

'Okay, okay.' Maggie had the wisdom to know when to call a halt. 'Anyway, it's nearly half-past seven; you'd better go and get dressed.'

Kim had just walked out of the shower when Maggie had knocked, and was still wearing her bathrobe with her wet hair bundled in a handtowel turban-style, and now she glanced at the sitting room clock in horror before flying out of the room, calling over her shoulder as she made for the cottage's narrow stairs, 'Melody's milk and biscuits are ready on a tray in the kitchen. I said you'd read to her while she eats her supper.'

'No problem.' Maggie continued to stare after her friend for a moment or two before walking through into the neat and sparkling kitchen, and her broad freckled face was anxious. No problem, she had said, but unless she was very much mistaken there was a problem of momentous proportions brewing here.

Kim was lovely, exquisitely lovely to look at, but more than that she was lovely inside where it counts. But vulnerable, painfully vulnerable, and she hid that vulnerability behind an armour that somehow this Lucas Kane had managed to penetrate—whether Kim acknowledged it or not. And that wasn't good.

Maggie frowned to herself as she reached for the tray and made her way upstairs. She'd have a good look at this tycoon who was so apparently irresistible tonight, and if she thought he was the type to give Kim the run-around—well, she'd just have a good look at him tonight and take it from there, she told herself stoutly, but her mouth was set in an uncharacteristically grim line and her expression was formidable.

Kim wasn't downstairs when Lucas knocked at the front door just before eight, so after warning Melody to stay in bed Maggie made her somewhat ponderous way to the front door.

'Good evening.' Lucas smiled at the dour-faced woman in the doorway. 'You must be Maggie. I'm Lucas Kane.' He held out a huge bunch of flowers as he added, 'These are for you, to say thanks for babysitting at such short notice.'

Maggie smiled back as she took the flowers—she could hardly do anything else, she told herself silently, when she experienced a moment's contrition at her easy capitulation, besides which she had to admit Lucas had quite taken her breath away—and managed to say, a little breathlessly for her, 'Come in, won't you? Kim will be down in a moment.'

'She's trying to dry her nails but they're taking *ages*.'

This last was from Melody who, unbeknown to both her mother and Maggie, had slid out of bed and was now perched at the top of the stairs, staring through the banisters at Lucas with great brown eyes.

'Are they?' As Maggie and Lucas glanced upward, Lucas grinned at the tiny miniature of Kim. 'Mine took ages, too,' he assured her solemnly.

'Silly.' Melody giggled and wriggled her small body. 'It's only ladies who paint their nails.'

'You're supposed to be in bed, young lady.' Maggie was flustered and it was a new feeling for her, one she didn't care for. 'Back you go and I'll be up in a minute to finish that story.'

'Here, take this before you go.' Lucas reached into the pocket of his overcoat and drew out a small wrapped package which he threw up to Melody, who caught it deftly. 'That's for being a good girl for your Aunt Maggie. You are going to be a good girl, aren't you?'

'Melody's always a good girl.' Maggie felt she had lost control of the situation somehow and she wasn't quite sure how it had happened.

'I'm sure she is.' Lucas smiled down at Maggie again, his voice soothing, and then as Melody shrieked her delight with the beautifully dressed little teddy bear the parcel had contained, he added quietly, 'You go up and see to her, Maggie. I'm fine, really. I'll just sit and wait for Kim.'

'Right.' Maggie stared at him, nonplussed and out of her depth. 'I'll just put the flowers in the kitchen.' She looked

down at the magnificent array of yellow roses, white car-
nations, baby's breath and freesias, and then, as she glanced
at Lucas again, she saw his mouth was twitching.

'I admit it, I'm trying to win you over,' he said softly,
reading her mind so aptly Maggie turned beetroot-red. 'I
need all the help I can get with Kim.'

'I…I'll put the flowers in water.' Maggie berated herself
as soon as she'd left the room for not seizing on such a
perfect opportunity to ask Lucas how he felt about Kim,
but somehow—now he was here in the flesh and a hundred
times more daunting than ever Kim had described—she
hadn't dared.

Which made her the wimp of the decade, she told herself
irritably as she hurried upstairs to Melody's pretty pink and
cream bedroom which she and Kim, along with Pete, had
decorated the first weekend Kim had moved into her new
house.

Just a few yards along the landing, Kim was surveying
herself in the full-length mirror in her bedroom. She hadn't
known what to wear—what did women wear for a date with
a multi-millionaire anyway? she thought with wry humour—but had finally put on one of the two new evening
outfits she had bought a couple of months before, courtesy
of Kane Electrical's clothing allowance.

The sleeveless olive-green silk and cashmere dress had
a matching waist-length cashmere jacket and had cost an
arm and a leg, but when Kim had seen it in one of the more
exclusive little shops in Cambridge she had known it was
eminently suitable for any evening function she might attend as Lucas's secretary. It was chic without being osten-
tatious, elegant and stylish, and fitted her like a dream. The
colour emphasised the striking contrast between her hair
and her eyes and brought out the honey-gold tone of her
skin to the extent she had gasped when she had first tried
the outfit on.

What would Lucas think when he saw her? She caught at the thought, refusing to let it have head room, but nevertheless the thrill of excitement the beautiful clothes had induced lingered in spite of herself, and as Kim applied a dab of perfume to each wrist and small crystal studs to her ears her hands were trembling.

She popped in to kiss Melody goodnight before she nerved herself to go downstairs, and as she stepped into the room her daughter's eyes widened appreciatively. 'You look so pretty, Mummy, like the princess in Aunty Maggie's story.'

'Thank you, precious.' Kim sat down on the edge of the bed and gathered the small body close, careless of the new outfit. Melody smelt of baby powder and her soft blonde hair was still slightly damp from her bath and curling slightly round the elfin face. Kim felt such a surge of love well up in her as her daughter's arms wound round her neck and Melody's lips pressed against hers that she closed her eyes against it, holding Melody against her heart for some seconds before she settled her daughter back under the duvet.

'You look stunning.' Maggie had been with her when she had bought the outfit, and her voice was wry as she added, 'But you'd look great in sackcloth and ashes, like I told you before.'

Kim smiled at her friend; she knew Maggie found her lack of confidence in her looks amazing but she couldn't help it. The years in the children's home followed by her disastrous marriage and Graham's mental abuse had damaged something deep in her psyche, and although she had fought back—and would continue to fight—she wasn't quite there yet.

But she looked good tonight. She gave a mental nod to the declaration as she stood up, her voice low as she said to Maggie, 'Well? What do you think?', inclining her head towards the door.

Maggie answered the unspoken question about Lucas by shaking her fingers as though they'd been burnt. 'Wow.' One word but it covered everything.

And then both women turned to the small figure in the bed in consternation as Melody said, her piping voice very clear and direct, '*I* think Lucas is scrumptious.' One of Melody's Christmas presents had been a video of the film *Chitty Chitty Bang Bang*, and 'scrumptious' was her new word for the moment and used for all sorts of good things.

But Lucas? Kim glanced at Maggie anxiously and Maggie shrugged, her voice dry as she said, 'Bright as a button, and serves us right for being so arrogant to think we could talk in code with Miss Muffet around.'

'I do, I think he's scrumptious.' Melody had caught the vibes concerning her new hero and wasn't having any of it. 'Look what Lucas brought me, Mummy.' She held up the little bear for Kim's inspection.

'Lovely, darling.'

'He brought me flowers.' Maggie's voice was magnificently expressionless.

'He did?' Kim eyed her helplessly. 'But I hadn't told him you'd be babysitting.'

'You might not have told him but he knew anyway.'

The two women stared at each other for another long moment and then Kim said, her tone one of resignation, 'I'd better go down.'

The sitting room door was open, and as Kim came down the stairs and reached the threshold, Lucas turned from his quiet contemplation of the garden and Kim received a bolt of electricity as the thickly lashed, curiously silver eyes looked at her. He didn't say a word for what seemed like an eternity; he just stared at her, the most strange expression on his hard, attractive face.

'Hello.' Kim attempted a smile but it was more a quiver of her lips.

'Hello.' It was very soft and very deep and made every nerve in Kim's body twang. 'You look...exquisitely lovely.'

'Thank you.' The intensity of his gaze was making her skin tingle and to combat the feeling, and the warm seductive spell that had settled over the last minute or two, Kim said evenly, 'It was nice of you to bring Maggie the flowers and to think of Melody but it wasn't necessary.'

'Meaning you didn't like it,' Lucas challenged pleasantly.

'I didn't say that.'

'You didn't have to.'

He seemed quite unconcerned and it rankled, badly. She stared at him, totally unaware of how her face was betraying her, and was further taken aback when he strolled over to her with lazy assuredness, taking her arm as he said, 'So, my prickly little secretary, ready for an evening with the big bad wolf? Do you have a coat? It's chilly outside.'

'It's in the hall.' She had stiffened at his touch and had seen his mouth tighten but she just couldn't help it. He was so...big.

The Aston Martin was crouching on Kim's short drive, looking quite incongruous in such humble surroundings, and she found herself taking several deep silent breaths as she slid into the car and waited for Lucas to join her after he had shut the passenger door.

'Have you eaten since lunchtime?'

'What?' Kim turned startled eyes to his dark face.

'Food.' His voice was patient now, overly so, and made her want to kick him. 'Has any passed your lips lately?'

'I had a little of the spaghetti bolognese I made for Melody's tea,' Kim said a trifle defensively. 'Just the last bit in the pan. There was too much to put on her plate.'

'Dangerous habit, that.' He slanted a mocking glance at her from under hooded lids. 'You'll get fat if you eat Melody's leftovers.'

'It wasn't exactly her leftovers,' Kim returned tightly. 'Besides, I was hungry.'

In actual fact, she had thought eating something might calm the flutters in her stomach the thought of the evening ahead had produced, but it hadn't worked.

'All to the good anyway; we shan't be eating until later.'

He started the engine as he spoke, nosing the car out of the small driveway and on to the quiet residential road beyond Kim's front garden.

Kim forced herself to sit absolutely still although every sense in her body was screaming. He was wearing an intoxicatingly delicious aftershave that was subtly sensual and made her want to lean over for a good deep lungful as she nuzzled the harsh—and, she had noticed, recently shaved—jawline.

She lifted her chin in defiance against herself and said carefully, 'We're having that talk first?'

'We're going to the theatre first,' Lucas said mildly.

'The theatre?'

It was almost in the nature of a screech and Lucas narrowed his eyes against it as he repeated, 'The theatre.'

'But…but you didn't say anything about the theatre.' She felt somehow that this was turning into a proper date, with this new slant on the evening.

'Look on it as a nice surprise,' Lucas said smoothly at the side of her, his eyes on the road ahead.

'I don't like surprises.' It was a touch petulant but Kim was past caring. How on earth had she come to be sitting here like this with Lucas Kane driving her to goodness knew where? she asked herself feverishly. He was as male as males went, and everything which cold logical common sense told her was dangerous. Strong and aggressive, with a darn sight too much sexual charisma and pull in the male-female department, not to mention hugely experienced and wealthy to boot.

'Stop panicking, Kim. I'm taking you to the theatre and then to dinner, not to show you my etchings.'

Her eyes shot to the dark profile but Lucas's face was unreadable.

She opened her mouth to deny the accusation and then shut it again. She couldn't win in a war of words with Lucas. Every time she attempted it she seemed to get herself into a worse tangle and he won another battle. Besides which—she bit her lip hard and concentrated fiercely on the dark road ahead—he was right. As usual.

Okay, so she couldn't compete with him mentally, and neither could she deny the effect he had on her physically, she told herself silently, but what she could do was to conduct herself with cool dignity and reserve throughout the evening. The ice maiden approach. Say little, observe much and rise to nothing.

The more she had got to know him, the more she had realised why Lucas chose his lovers from women with careers as similarly high-powered to his own. He was an intimidatingly intelligent individual; he would require mental stimulation from any companion he invited into his bed as well as physical gratification. She wasn't dumb—even though Graham had tried to persuade her otherwise—but neither did she have what those sort of women had.

She had always liked the idea of a career, but she knew herself well enough to recognise that for her family and home would always come first. She didn't want to be up with the cream of the high-fliers—knowing all the latest deals, the latest gossip, having a finger on the pulse and acting ruthlessly and with absolute focus when she had to. And that was the sort of women Lucas gravitated towards.

She was just a change from his usual diet, a passing fancy; he'd find her infinitely boring after a time.

So... She narrowed dark eyes at the brightly lit streets as they reached the heart of the city. She would just be herself but with a great deal of reserve. And by the end of the evening he'd probably be champing at the bit to get her home.

Her soft mouth drooped unknowingly.

The theatre was splendid and their seats were in the stalls with an excellent view of the stage, but Kim was hardly conscious of her surroundings.

Like her, Lucas had dressed up—in his case, a black dinner-jacket and tie—and when he had removed his overcoat in the foyer she had had to force her eyes away with relentless determination when she realised she was ogling him, pretending to admire the elaborately decorated walls and ceiling instead, her cheeks burning.

Once in their seats she buried herself in the programme Lucas had bought her, steeling herself to show no reaction when his thigh briefly brushed hers as he adjusted his long limbs in the limited leg-room.

He leant over her slightly as the cast-list swam and moved before her eyes. 'Have you seen this particular company before?' he asked easily. His cool relaxed tone further evidence to Kim that she was the one with the problem.

'No—no, I haven't.'

'They're good.'

'Right.' As he settled back into his own seat Kim expelled her breath in a silent relieved sigh and prayed for the performance to begin.

How could you be surrounded by people and yet feel as if the rest of the world wasn't there? she asked herself desperately. She didn't *want* to feel like this. It was too disturbing. She didn't want to be with Lucas Kane. *He* was too disturbing.

'Stop frowning; people will think we've had a fight.'

Her eyes snapped sideways and met the mocking silver gaze head on. 'You're my boss, I'm your secretary; having a fight isn't an option,' Kim said primly.

'Is that so?' Lucas contemplated the statement. 'Then what happened after I kissed you?' he asked interestedly. 'Correct me if I'm wrong, but if that wasn't a fight I wouldn't want to be around you when you're really mad.'

Kim eyed him severely. She didn't want to be reminded of that kiss and she suspected Lucas knew it. 'That was just setting the record straight.' And look where it had got her!

'The record being that you do not want a sexual relationship with any man ever again,' Lucas murmured softly. 'Which, of course, is too ridiculous to take seriously.'

'Ridiculous or not, that's the way I feel.' It was a sharp snap, all her earlier resolutions of keeping calm and distant blown to the wind.

'No, you don't.' There was triumph in the silver eyes. 'You want me, Kim. Your lips and your body told me that this morning.'

'*Lucas.*' Kim glanced round nervously.

'And sooner or later it will happen,' he continued silkily. 'You know that as well as I do; that's why you've been as jumpy as a cat on a hot tin roof from the first day you came to work for me.'

'It won't happen, Lucas.' Her eyes had darkened to ebony, and Lucas experienced a moment of intense irritation at the stubborn set of her soft mouth. 'I have Melody; she's the only person I need in my life.'

'Melody is a wonderful little girl but she's a child.' He was careful not to let any of his anger sound in his voice. 'I'm talking about a normal healthy relationship between two adults of the opposite sex.'

'If such a thing exists.' It was out before she even

thought about it, and she felt her heart thud with horror at what she had unwittingly revealed. How was it he made her say things like that? she asked herself feverishly. Made her face things she didn't even know she felt herself?

'Oh, it exists, all right.' His voice was very soft and his eyes piercing on her flushed unhappy face. 'And when it's good it's the greatest thing on earth.'

'I wouldn't know anything about that.' It was very stiff and cool. 'And frankly I don't want to.'

'Yes, you do.' He refused to accept her self-denial. 'But you're too scared, too locked up in yourself to admit it. You want me to hold you, Kim, to kiss you, taste you, ravish you. You want me to take you to heaven and back, to feel me inside you while you lie naked in my arms.'

'Lucas, stop it. You can't say things like that here.' She was shattered, but more by the dangerous desire his soft deep voice was invoking than anything else.

'Why? No one can hear us.' He was so close she felt enveloped in his maleness, his scent, his warmth, and she was trembling. She couldn't help it.

'Please, Lucas...'

'I want you, Kim. I want you more than I've ever wanted any woman in my life and after this morning I know you want me, too. I'm not going to let you deny us both.'

The arrival of further couples at the side of them, corresponding with the theatre lights fading and the start of the play, effectively finished any further conversation, but Kim continued to shake for the first ten minutes of Tennessee Williams's *Suddenly Last Summer*, and in spite of the potent and riveting nature of the play she couldn't seem to let her mind give it the attention it deserved.

The bar was crowded at the interval but Kim didn't mind that; it cut out the chance of any more intimate conversation.

She concentrated on sipping her glass of white wine with

what she hoped was seen as cool aplomb, but with Lucas's arm draped casually round her waist and his lean hard frame pressed against her in the crush of human bodies, the composure was only on the surface.

In just a few hours Lucas had managed to completely alter the tenor of their association from formal employer and employee to... Her mind jerked to a halt. To what, exactly? she asked herself silently. Well, whatever it was, it didn't matter. She had to get back to how it had been and as quickly as possible.

'You're frowning again.' His lips brushed her ear as he whispered against the silk of her hair and she felt the impact right down to her toes.

'Am I?' She looked at him out of the corner of her eye but refused to be drawn further.

'Uh-huh. And I dare bet you were thinking of me,' he drawled affably.

'Surprising though it may seem, I'm not always thinking of you.'

'Something I intend to rectify from now on,' said Lucas firmly.

Kim took another sip of her wine and prayed for the wit and courage to put him in his place. It didn't come. She adjusted her position slightly as a large plump woman on the other side of her who was drenched in a particularly sickly-sweet perfume trod on her left foot, but the manoeuvre only had the effect of emphasising that Lucas wasn't quite so cool and controlled as he looked as she came into contact with his thighs.

The betrayal of his body startled her into looking straight into his face and the silver eyes were waiting for her, his mouth twisted in a crooked grin that told her he was fully aware of her thoughts. 'I told you I wanted you, Kim,' he said gently against her ear again, his warm breath causing frissons of sensation in every part of her. 'And a cold shower isn't an option here.'

She knew her cheeks were burning and wished with all her heart that she was one of the sophisticated, blasé, worldly-wise women he was used to, women who would have a light amusing comment on their tongue to defuse such a situation without any awkwardness—but she wasn't. And then, as Lucas reached behind him and placed his empty glass on a shelf running along the length of the wall, he moved her into the circle of his arms, his hands resting possessively on her waist.

'Incredible woman,' he whispered softly against her forehead, his warm lips caressing her as he spoke. 'Defiant and angry one minute, shy and bewildered the next. I don't know one other woman who blushes like you do. Sensual and all woman in my arms and then as cold as a beautiful ice sculpture. You fascinate me, Kim. Do you know that?'

'I don't want to fascinate you,' she said desperately, whilst knowing—with a feeling of overwhelming panic— that that wasn't quite the truth. Which made her crazy, insane, because getting involved with Lucas would mean emotional suicide for sure.

'Perhaps that's part of what drew me at first,' Lucas murmured thoughtfully, almost to himself, as he leant back slightly in order to hold her drowning eyes. 'The world is full of gold-diggers, Kim, or men and women who chose their partners for the kudos reflected on them. Esteem, renown, furthering one's reputation or career—it's the name of the game.'

'Not my game.' She tried to extricate herself from his arms but he didn't seem to notice, and then, as she broke eye contact, she looked at his mouth and her heart seemed to stand still. It was a hard, faintly stern mouth—even when he was being gentle, the way he was now—and devastatingly sexy.

'No, I know that.' His brow creased in a quizzical ruffle.
'Sometimes you seem as young as Melody, and yet the very
fact of her existence proves you are not what you seem.
You've been married, borne a child. You're a mother, a
single parent who provides for her family.' There was a
faintly whimsical note to his voice, as though he couldn't
believe what he was saying, and although she felt she
should feel insulted Kim couldn't summon up the necessary
anger.

'Lots of people are different underneath,' she managed
evasively, vitally aware of his hands idly caressing her slender waist and the massiveness of his shoulders and broad
chest. They were creating a whole host of feelings she
could well have done without.

'Maybe, but usually for the worst,' Lucas responded
drily.

'That might be the case with me.' She had spoken lightly
but the root was in her fragile self-esteem, and instead of
the witty or cynical answer she was expecting Lucas said
nothing for a few moments, his eyes narrowing on her
lovely face.

'If he wasn't dead, I'd want to kill him.'

It was like a punch in the chest and tension shot through
every part of her body at the look in his eyes. She froze,
becoming stiff and unyielding in his arms, and Lucas swore
silently to himself for going too fast.

But then she slowly relaxed again, brushing a wisp of
hair from her thick fringe out of her eyes as she said, very
quietly, so quietly he had to lower his head slightly to hear
her, 'He used to say that to me, that he wanted to kill me,
towards the end. He knew I wanted to leave him and he
used to threaten—'

'What?' Lucas was amazed she was talking like this and
scared to say anything in case it drove her back in her shell.

'He used to say he would kill Melody first, then me. That

he would find me wherever I went, hunt us down. He...he was unbalanced when he was drinking, violent, capable of anything. And then other times, when he was sober, he would take Melody to the park and act like a normal father. But I could never relax. One time he went out sober and came back and I could smell the drink on his breath. He wasn't drunk, but he'd been drinking when he was supposed to be looking after her.'

She raised agonised eyes to his horrified face as he expelled a long hard breath.

'I wouldn't let him go out alone with her after that; I wouldn't let her out of my sight for a minute. He was becoming too unpredictable,' Kim said flatly.

'Did he go anywhere for help, professional help?' Lucas asked softly.

Kim shook her head, her eyes cloudy and dark. 'Graham wouldn't acknowledge he'd got a problem,' she said bitterly. 'It was me who was at fault, according to him. I was boring, a kill-joy; he used to—' She stopped abruptly, suddenly aware she was saying too much. There were some things, secret things, she had sworn she would never tell a living soul.

'He used to?'

'It doesn't matter.' She was retreating from him but there was nothing he could do about it in the middle of a theatre bar, Lucas told himself silently.

'Could I have another glass of wine?' Kim finished the last of the clear white liquid in one gulp and held the glass out to him with a brittle smile. She didn't really want another drink but she had to do something to break the curiously intimate bubble his arms had woven round her, a bubble that had made her reveal far more than she had intended.

In the last few minutes before the bell rang for the second half Lucas kept the conversation light and amusing, and

Kim tried to respond in kind, but inwardly she was as tight as a coiled spring.

Now that the spell his nearness had evoked was broken she couldn't believe how she had spoken to him—*him*, Lucas, the one person in all the world she needed to keep at a distance. She didn't want him to know anything about her life—past or present—she told herself feverishly. He had power enough over her as it was.

In spite of all her misgivings and self-recrimination, Kim found herself enjoying the second half. And then the lights rose and they were making their way out to the car, the damp chilly air after the hot-house warmth of the theatre making Kim shiver on the steps of the building.

'Cold?' Lucas didn't wait for an answer, drawing her into his side with a practised ease that seemed perfectly natural and which made Kim feel she would be overly crass if she objected to the arm round her shoulders. But it was too cosy, too 'coupleish' to be anything but acutely disturbing.

The meal, at a wonderful little Italian restaurant a short drive from the theatre, was delicious, and contrary to all her expectations Kim found herself relaxing enough to enjoy the excellent food.

Lucas seemed to have metamorphosed into yet another of his many selves and this one, a convivial and charming dinner companion, was sufficiently non-threatening to be, if not quite comfortable, then certainly agreeable.

He didn't mention her disclosure from their talk at the theatre during the meal, nor yet on the drive home, and Kim felt too emotionally drained to bring up the original purpose of their dinner date. Anxious as she was to set their relationship on the right footing again, any further discussion about it was beyond her for the moment.

She stared out into the dark night as the Aston Martin purred through misty, deserted streets.

Lucas was the most confusing, exasperating, arrogant, authoritarian man she'd ever met, she told herself crossly, painfully conscious of every tiny movement from the hard male body at her side.

Since they had started the drive home he hadn't said more than a word or two, his attention seemingly concentrated on his driving, but the silence was neither quiet or restful—as far as Kim was concerned. In fact the car seemed to vibrate with a throbbing current which was setting Kim's teeth on edge, as though fingernails were rasping down a slate blackboard.

She was feeling horribly vulnerable for a whole host of reasons: all she had revealed about her past, the fact that she had—despite all her efforts to the contrary—enjoyed being with him, but most of all the knowledge that soon— very soon—he would kiss her again. But she could control the kiss this time, she assured herself vehemently. Of course she could. Whatever Lucas expected, she would make sure it was a polite thank you type of embrace, a brief touching of their lips before she got out of the car and she was not—*she was not*—going to ask him in for coffee.

With each mile that passed Kim could feel herself getting tenser and tenser, and then they were cruising down her street and the Aston Martin nosed its way across the crossover and into the short pebbled drive in front of the cottage.

She was home. Kim took a deep breath, the courteous little speech she had rehearsed for the last ten minutes hovering on her tongue, and then she found the wind completely taken out of her sails when Lucas said, his tone even and pleasant, 'That was a great evening, Kim. Thank Maggie again for me, would you, for helping out with Melody?'

'Yes, yes, I will.' Was that it? That couldn't be it, *surely*?

She watched in something approaching disbelief as Lucas opened his door and walked round the wetly gleam-

ing bonnet, and then her door was open and his hand was
helping her to alight.

'Good night, Kim.' The brushing of her lips was as brief
as ever she had determined earlier, but it was *Lucas* calling
the tune and controlling events.

'Good night.'

The word was still on her lips when he turned and
walked back to the car, opening his door and sliding into
the leather interior with a cool smile.

How dared he? After all he had said, how *dared* he not
kiss her? she raged silently. Not that she would have allowed the sort of kiss they had shared earlier, not for a
minute, but how dared he not try?

She was still standing there, seething with hurt pride and
sheer astonishment, when the car backed out of the drive
and on to the road beyond. And then it was gone, in a flash
of sleek metal and bright lights, and the damp, chilly night
enfolded her in its shadowy darkness.

Why hadn't he kissed her? She touched her mouth with
a bemused hand. *Really* kissed her? She glanced up into
the night sky but the dense thick rainclouds held no answers. Didn't he like her any more? Perhaps he had been
bored tonight, the way she'd wished earlier; they said you
should be careful what you wished for.

Of course, it was all to the good. She drew in a lungful
of cold air that smelt of wet earth and vegetation, and bit
her lip against the urge to cry. It really was. This way she
was saved the embarrassing necessity of having to rebuff
his advances, to fight him off.

Fight him off! She smiled bitterly. He hadn't been able
to get away quickly enough. Well, that was the end of that.
She nodded to the thought and then said it out loud, her
breath a white cloud in the cold air. And she was glad. She
was really, really glad. She only felt this sick churning in
her stomach because of the rich food, that was all.

She stood for a few moments more until she became aware her coat was enshrouded with tiny droplets from the misty rain and turned abruptly, squaring her shoulders as she walked over to the front door and searched her small handbag for her key.

It would be work tomorrow as usual.

CHAPTER SEVEN

KIM spent a wretched night tossing and turning and finally gave up all hope of sleep at four in the morning, padding quietly down to the kitchen and making herself a steaming cup of hot chocolate.

She drank it curled up in one of the armchairs with just the dim light from a table lamp lighting the sitting room, and the dying glow from the embers of the fire providing a little warmth.

She didn't want to feel like this. It was a silent wail but none the less anguished for it. She didn't want to let any man under her skin ever again. But somehow...somehow Lucas had managed to turn her world upside down in the five months in which she'd worked for him. She had been fighting this strange attraction, this almost consuming fascination from day one, if she was being truthful.

She should never have accepted the post as secretary to Lucas, it had been foolhardy—madness. But then she wouldn't have had this lovely home, had a chance to clear her debts once and for all and to take charge of her life, and Melody's, again, would she? she argued back.

And she could get a handle on this; it just needed discipline, and of course it would be a whole lot easier now if he had decided she wasn't worth the effort.

The thought hit her hard in the chest and she bowed her head over the mug, her eyes desolate. She was going crazy, here, she told herself miserably. She had to pull herself together. She would never contemplate exposing herself and Melody to the risk of another disastrous relationship, she knew that deep inside, so whether Lucas wanted her or not was immaterial.

After another cup of chocolate Kim decided she had moped enough. She set her face resolutely, pulled out the ironing board and tackled the pile of ironing she had been trying to ignore for days. That finished, she fetched out her baking tins and set about making one of the rich chocolate cakes Melody loved so much, followed by a cheese and bacon flan for their tea later that day.

It was light outside by the time she had finished, and after clearing up the kitchen she ran herself a hot bath and luxuriated in the warm bubbles for over half an hour, relishing that she had plenty of time for once.

After washing her hair and applying a rich conditioner she let it dry naturally whilst she creamed every inch of her skin, pampering herself in a way she hadn't done for ages.

She wanted to look her absolute best today. She didn't question why it was so important, it just was.

Once in her cream and pine bedroom, Kim contemplated the contents of her wardrobe thoughtfully. She needed to radiate cool control and efficiency. Never mind she didn't feel it, she told herself bracingly, half the population got through on a wing and a prayer at some point in their lives, and this was her point. She was not going to creep into the office this morning like a small whipped puppy—she was going to be the dignified, mature, capable woman she really was. Simple.

By the time every item of clothing was strewn over the bed, Kim was panicking. It was time to get Melody up for school and normally by now she was dressed, perfectly groomed and had prepared their breakfast.

'Calm, girl. Calm.' She spoke out loud before shutting her eyes and breathing in and out deeply a few times. 'This is just a normal working day. That's all it is.'

'Who are you talking to, Mummy?' Melody had poked her head round the half-open bedroom door and now Kim saw great liquid brown eyes surveying her unblinkingly. 'And why is that big heap of clothes on your bed?'

'Mummy's having a sort-out.'

'Can I take Edward to school to show Kerry and Susan?' Kim saw the small bear Lucas had bought her was tucked under one pyjama-clad arm where no doubt he'd spent the night. It did not help Kim's current state of mind an iota.

'I don't think so, darling. What if he got lost or dirty?' Kim said as calmly as she could. 'Why don't you put him with all your other cuddly toys and then he'll be here when you get home tonight?'

Melody considered the suggestion with a tilt of her blonde head. 'I'll put him on my pillow,' she decided firmly, 'and then all the others will know he's the boss.'

Kim smiled weakly. It seemed to sum everything up somehow.

Once she had chivvied Melody to have a quick wash and get dressed, Kim nipped downstairs and prepared their breakfast of cereal and toast, before flying upstairs again and reaching for the nearest item of clothing on top of the pile.

She would clear everything away when she got home, she decided feverishly, dressing hastily before brushing her hair through. The conditioner had done its work, and her golden blonde locks hung like a shining silk curtain to her shoulders, her fringe almost shimmering in the artificial light over the mirror.

She could wear her hair loose today. It was a full ten seconds before she realised she was seriously considering the thought, and for all the wrong reasons. She didn't *want* Lucas to be attracted to her, she told herself vehemently, or consider what he had missed by not attempting to take things further last night. She didn't want him in her life, not in a personal sense. He was too manipulative by half, and far too charismatic—he had already won Melody over, hook, line and sinker, and Maggie had been distinctly mellowed by that outrageously extravagant gesture with the flowers.

She glared at the reflection in the mirror before pulling her hair back so ferociously not a wisp dared escape, and once it was secure she applied her usual light make-up and stood back to survey the result.

Her neatly tailored suit in a sedate navy blue was smart and practical, and the cream blouse underneath buttoned right up to the neck with a demure stand-up collar. She looked every inch the executive secretary, and that was *all* she wanted to look like.

She would go into work as normal this morning, perform her duties to the best of her ability and return home satisfied in the knowledge she had earnt every penny of the excellent salary.

And if—and, going by Lucas's departure last night, the if was huge—he should ask her for another date she would refuse, politely and firmly, and stand her ground this time, come hell or high water.

Kim drove into the large car park of Kane Electrical at her usual time and then stared in surprise at the empty space next to her reserved spot. No Aston Martin meant no Lucas.

The reason for this became clear when she reached her office. There was a cream envelope on her desk with her name written on it in Lucas's unmistakable bold black script. The note the envelope contained was brief and to the point:

Kim, my father contacted me just before midnight from the hospital in Florida where they'd taken him and my mother after the car he was driving burst a tyre at high speed. They have a few broken bones between them but I understand the tree that was foolish enough to get in the way fared worse. I'm flying over to check how things are but hope to return tomorrow. Their telephone number is in the address book in the left-hand drawer of my desk if you need me.

There followed a list of instructions about the pile of work under the envelope, followed by his name. And that was all.

Kim stared at the writing for some time, her mind swirling and her conscience telling her she was dreadful, *awful*, to think about the formal tenor of the letter at a time like this.

His parents were in hospital and he was obviously worried enough to go shooting off halfway across the world; he probably hadn't had any sleep or food or anything else, and here was she worrying that the letter seemed…cold, off-hand. And why shouldn't it be, anyway? she reprimanded herself in the next instant. She was his secretary, that was all. *That was all she was.*

The day dragged interminably, and whether it was due to the sleepless night she had endured or the amount of correspondence she doggedly worked through Kim wasn't sure, but by the time she left the building her head was thumping and she was so exhausted she went straight to bed as soon as Melody had gone to sleep.

The next morning she tried to ignore the anticipation that was sending little frissons of sensation down her spine on the drive to Kane Electrical, but as the day progressed and there was no word from Lucas Kim found herself leaping to answer the phone each time it rang, and holding her breath every time she heard voices in the corridor outside.

Five o'clock did eventually make its appearance. Kim

slid the cover over her word processor and refused to let the cloud made up of hurt and disappointment and a hundred other confused emotions besides settle over her.

She was glad all this had happened right now, she told herself firmly, as she took the lift down to reception. She might, she just *might* have been foolish enough to take on board some of the things Lucas had said and done if this hadn't showed her it was all surface level. The wanting her, his quiet gentleness and compassion when she'd revealed a little of how it had been with Graham, the way he'd set out to charm her and make her laugh during their meal— oh, a million things!

She sighed irritably. She still had a whole truckload of ghosts to lay before she could consider herself free from the past, and confronting some of those personal demons was going to be hard enough as it was.

Yes, this was definitely all for the best. When Lucas arrived back in the office no doubt he would resume the easy working relationship he had adopted before that disastrous kiss, and everything would be back to normal. Whatever that was.

When she and Melody got out of the car a little while later, Kim stood for a moment or two on the drive just looking about her.

It was the first day of April, and the spring evening was cool and mellow with a hint of woodsmoke wafting in the lazy breeze that ruffled the branches of the silver birch at the corner of the front garden.

Underneath the tree a host of sweetly coloured crocuses and primroses were in full bloom, and although the pebbled drive made up the rest of the garden the whole effect was pretty and pleasing. And it was hers, all hers, Kim thought soberly. And she had a great job, and she and Melody were healthy and financially secure for the first time in years— everything was terrific.

So why, in view of all that, did she have such a feeling of heaviness on her? Kim asked herself silently. There was a lead weight on her heart and an underlying feeling of restlessness she could well do without.

This was further enhanced when the telephone rang just after she and Melody had finished tea. It was Maggie, and from the tone of her friend's voice Kim knew immediately something was wrong.

'I'm taking that job in America for six months, Kim.' Maggie had told her a few weeks before about the wonderful offer from a wealthy businessman who wanted Maggie to design and oversee the interiors of both his new apartment in New York and a sumptuous beach house in California. But Maggie had been unsure about leaving England—and more particularly Pete—for such a long stretch, and had been dithering as to whether to take the commission. 'I leave after the weekend.'

'It's a brilliant opportunity, Maggie.' Kim repeated the words she had used when Maggie had first told her about the venture. 'What made up your mind to accept?'

'Pete,' said Maggie flatly. 'I've had enough, Kim. I've told him he's a free agent while I'm gone but if he wants me when I come back it means the whole hog—full commitment, and that includes marriage. I want children, Kim, and soon. We've been together long enough for him to make up his mind one way or the other, and this seems like the perfect time for him to sort himself out. If he can't do without me, great. If it's all over when I come home, so be it. This is the short, sharp shock treatment you suggested once.'

'Are you sure?' Kim asked anxiously. Maggie worshipped the ground Pete walked on.

'No, I'm frightened to death he'll pull the plug, if you want to know,' Maggie said dejectedly, 'but I can't carry on the way we are, either. It's killing me, Kim. We've agreed no contact, no letters or phone calls for the whole of the six months, so it's really make or break.'

They talked some more and after Kim had replaced the receiver she continued sitting at the foot of the stairs, staring into space.

She'd miss Maggie, and so would Melody, but she felt in her spirit Maggie was doing the right thing. It was a gamble, but then everything in life carried some sort of risk.

She frowned suddenly, aware her mind was trying to tell her something she couldn't grasp. And then the doorbell rang.

Kim glanced at her watch. Seven o'clock. Who on earth was calling at seven o'clock? she asked herself wearily. It had to be a salesman of some kind or other—the only other person who would pop round was Maggie and she'd only just got off the phone to her. She hoped it wasn't one of the more persistent individuals, that was all. She didn't feel like doing battle tonight.

She pulled herself up from the bottom stair and walked across the hall, opening the door with a polite refusal already hovering on her lips. *'Lucas!'* She could feel the colour pouring into her cheeks but she couldn't help it.

'Hello, Kim.'

'But you're in America,' she said stupidly.

'Am I?' He smiled. A tired smile. 'Clever me.'

'I mean, I thought you were in America,' she corrected quickly, suddenly hotly aware of the old jeans and skinny-rib jumper she had pulled on before making tea.

'Can I come in?'

She could feel the intensity of his gaze on her hair, which she had brushed out when she'd changed and was wearing loose on her shoulders, and her blush deepened. 'Oh, yes. I'm sorry. Of course, come in.' She was so flustered she nearly fell over her own feet as she backed away from the door, and then Melody emerged from the sitting room like a small bullet, her tiny face all lit up.

'Lucas!' With a total lack of inhibition Melody ran over to him and smiled up into the hard rugged face. 'Have you come to see me?' she asked trustingly.

'That I have.'

With his gaze now on the small figure of her daughter Kim was able to really look at him, and she saw the harsh face had a grey tinge of exhaustion and he looked utterly done in.

'Good,' Melody declared happily. 'Mummy and me are doing a jigsaw I had for Christmas. You can help if you like. It's *very* hard,' she added with a small frown.

'Darling, Mr Kane—Lucas—is tired,' Kim said quickly.

'But not too tired to try my hand at the jigsaw,' Lucas put in swiftly, holding out his arm to Melody, who took his hand immediately and dragged him off to the sitting room.

The jigsaw was lying on a big tray on the rug in front of the fire, and Kim watched with something approaching disbelief as her dignified and illustrious boss shrugged off his suit jacket and loosened his tie before squatting down next to Melody on the floor.

The light caught the shining blue-black jet of his hair and the fragile fairness of Melody's waves, emphasising the contrast between them, and for a moment Kim felt such a sense of panic she wanted to run across the room and snatch Melody up in her arms.

'Would…would you like a drink?' she asked helplessly from the doorway.

'I'd love one. Black coffee, please.' Lucas turned round and looked at her as he spoke, and the flickering glow from the fire picked out the lines of strain round his mouth and eyes.

He was dead beat. Kim stared at him for a second more

and then heard her voice asking, 'Have you eaten? I can rustle up something, if you like?'

He looked at her quietly for a moment. 'That would be great, Kim. Thank you.'

'Are your parents all right?' Too late she remembered she hadn't asked after them, but that was the trouble with Lucas, she told herself crossly. All coherent thought seemed to fly out of the window when he was around.

'They'll live.' It was dry. 'Dad is suffering more from the tongue-lashing Mum gave him than his broken leg and torn muscles. He always tends to drive too fast and she's sure that contributed to the accident.'

It seemed strange hearing him refer to his parents as Mum and Dad, somehow, and Kim didn't like the feeling the warmth in his voice engendered either. She didn't want to think of him as a loving son; it made him that touch more human and that was dangerous.

As Melody claimed Lucas's attention by tugging on his sleeve Kim said hastily, 'I'll get that coffee,' and shut the sitting room door quickly.

She stood still for a moment in the kitchen, aware her heart was pounding. He was here, he'd come. What did that mean? Her heart gave a mighty kick and she shut her eyes tightly, but that only painted the picture of Lucas—his shirt taut across muscled shoulders and his long legs crossed Buddha-fashion as he sat next to the tiny figure of Melody—more vividly across the screen of her mind.

Food. With unconscious drama she raised her hands and opened her fingers wide. Concentrate on the food, Kim, she told herself silently. She knew where she was with that.

At half-past seven Kim served up pork chops with lemon and herbs, and new potatoes and baby carrots and peas for Lucas, whisking Melody out of the room at the same time so Lucas could eat his food in peace whilst Melody had her bath and got into her pyjamas.

'This looks delicious. Thank you.'

The soft deep voice stopped Kim just as she was about to shut the sitting room door again and she turned, indicating for Melody to continue up the stairs, before she glanced back at Lucas and said, her smile brittle, 'There's either spicy apple, date and sesame loaf to follow or a piece of the chocolate cake Melody likes if you'd prefer.'

'Home-made chocolate cake?' It was almost winsome.

Kim nodded carefully.

'It's been years since I had home-made chocolate cake,' Lucas murmured appreciatively.

'Chocolate cake it is, then.'

After she shut the door Kim found she had to lean against it for a full thirty seconds. He was too sexy, she told herself despairingly. Too sexy by half. How did he manage to look so broodingly tough and little boy lost at the same time?

And she hadn't asked why he was here. She hadn't even acted as though a boss appearing on his secretary's doorstep at seven in the evening was unusual. She'd just simply offered him coffee and then proceeded to cook him a meal. Barmy. This man was sending her stark-staring barmy.

Once Melody was bathed and in bed Kim left her drawing a picture with her new set of pencils, after promising her she'd return and read her a story in a few minutes after she had fixed Lucas's dessert.

She heated the large slice of chocolate fudge cake just the slightest in the microwave, the way she did for Melody, and served it with a generous dollop of fresh cream, carrying it through to the sitting room quickly.

Lucas was sitting staring into the fire as she opened the door, his elbows on his knees and the empty plate at his side, and she noticed immediately he had taken his tie off and rolled up his shirt sleeves. The aura of masculinity was overwhelming, and Kim felt her stomach tighten.

'I should have rung before I came round,' he said

abruptly, rising to his feet at her entry into the dimly lit room.

What did he expect her to say to that? They looked at each other for a second, and then Kim said quietly, 'Why didn't you?'

'Because you would have put me off coming, said you'd see me tomorrow at the office, and I couldn't wait that long.'

He had moved closer to her as he had spoken, taking the plate from her suddenly nerveless fingers and placing it on a chair before straightening again and towering over her, his tall lean body hard and uncompromising and his silver-grey eyes registering the shocked surprise on her face.

'Lucas—'

'For the last forty-eight hours all I've done is to tell myself what a damn fool I was not to kiss you when I had the chance,' he growled softly. 'To hell with doing the honourable thing and giving you time. I need you, Kim.'

'Lucas, please—'

He caught the last breathless word with his lips, his mouth taking hers in a kiss that was all fire and passion, a kiss which rocked Kim to the core. But then almost immediately the ruthless control he exerted in every other area of his life slotted into place, and he was caressing her lips with small, sweet kisses as he moulded her against him.

His tongue rippled along her teeth and Kim shivered her response, barely aware that her hands had lifted to his muscular shoulders where her fingers rose further to tangle in the short, spiky black hair above his shirt collar.

His hands moved in slow exploration down the length of her trembling body with exquisitely controlled sensuality, and Kim found herself kissing him back with a hunger that matched his. She could hear little guttural moans but at first she didn't realise they were coming from deep in her throat, and even when the knowledge dawned she couldn't do anything about it.

She could feel the play of muscles beneath the silk of his shirt when she let her hands roam over the hard expanse of his powerful back, and the scent of him—that delicious, intoxicating mixture of expensive aftershave and pure male—was adding to the wild pleasure sweeping her senses.

His body was magnificent. The height and breadth of him was all around her, consuming in its maleness. *He* was magnificent. And the primitive raw excitement he induced when he so much as touched her was magnificent too. She had never imagined human beings could feel something as elemental as this.

'You're so beautiful,' he murmured huskily against her hungry mouth. 'Incredibly, fantastically beautiful.'

His lips moved to the silky hollow of her throat and she arched back her head, the thick fall of her hair like a shimmering curtain. She could feel the hot hardness of his erection against the softness of her belly and knew he was hugely aroused, but her emotion was one of fierce pride and power that she could make this man, this hard, ruthless, cold man, shake with passion.

And then they both heard it from the bedroom upstairs; a small but determined voice calling, 'Mummy, Mummy. I want you to read my story *now*.'

He raised his head very slowly and only after a trail of kisses ending at her half-open mouth. 'Saved by the bell?' he murmured quizzically against the smooth flushed skin of her cheek.

She stared at him, her eyes huge and seemingly unable to tear themselves away from the carved lines of his mouth and the dark stubble of beard on his chin. 'Your...your dessert,' she managed faintly. 'I came to give you your dessert.'

'It looks good enough to eat,' he said softly, and they both knew he wasn't talking about the cake.

'I need to go.' She gestured vaguely with one hand but still without taking her eyes off his hard, handsome face. 'Melody is waiting for me.'

He smiled, dropping a warm, featherlike kiss on the tip of her nose but without loosening his hold of her by the slightest. 'I know how she feels,' he said huskily. 'I feel like I've been waiting for you all of my life. I came straight from the airport tonight and if you hadn't been here I'd have camped outside until you came back. How come you've done that to me, woman?'

There was a note of real bewilderment in his throaty voice that almost made Kim smile. Almost. But now his mouth had left hers reality was rushing in, and with it the knowledge of how close she had been to losing control. Who was she kidding? she chided herself savagely in the next instant. Her control had been nonexistent. If it hadn't been for Melody calling...

'Lucas, you don't know me.' She tried to prise herself out of his arms as she spoke.

'The hell I don't.' It was soft and intent. 'What do you think the last five months have been all about? I know you and you know me, Kim. Don't try and kid yourself. We've spent most of the last one hundred and fifty-odd days together, damn it.'

'But not intimately,' she blurted out confusedly.

'I'm more than willing to rectify that at the earliest opportunity.'

'You know how I feel,' she muttered weakly, managing to move away from him as Melody's voice called again.

'Yes, I do,' he said with deadly certainty. 'And it's quite different to what you're *telling* me, isn't it, Kim?'

'No.' The protest was weak and the silver-grey eyes reflected their recognition of it.

'You want me, Kim, and I want you. It's as simple as that.'

'Nothing is as simple as that,' she shot back shakily. 'You've got no idea, have you? You think falling in and out of bed is just a grown-up game but it's not. It's not! I'm not like that.'

'Like what?' he bit back angrily, his face straightening and becoming as severe as the wintry hue of his eyes. 'I'm not suggesting a one-night stand, for crying out loud. And while we're on the subject, promiscuity has never been a habit of mine, in case you're wondering—neither have I ever fallen in or out of anywhere, to my knowledge!'

'I didn't mean...' Her voice trailed away as he surveyed her from narrowed unblinking eyes. 'Look, I have to go up to Melody.' She pointed to the cake with a trembling hand. 'Eat your cake.'

She heard him mutter something very rude as she turned and escaped from the room, but she didn't stop in her headlong flight.

Melody was all pouts and frowns when Kim entered her daughter's bedroom, but after establishing that no, Lucas could not come and read her story, and yes, Kim would stay with her until she was asleep, Melody snuggled down in bed and was asleep before the story was finished.

What had she done? Kim sat in the shadowed bedroom watching Melody as she slept, her eyes lingering on the small rosebud mouth and the thick lashes on the porcelain skin, the way Melody's fine silky hair tumbled over the pillow like spun gold.

She had to tell him, as soon as she went downstairs, that she wanted him to leave. Moreover, that if their relationship couldn't be constrained to a purely platonic working association, then she would have to leave Kane Electrical.

Her heart gave a massive thud and then raced for a few seconds, reminding her—as if she needed it—that the thought made her feel sick. But she would do it, she told herself firmly. This was survival. He'd got too close.

She wasn't quite sure when and how it had happened but it didn't really matter now. The end result was the same. She had let him work himself into her life and that meant the potential of pain and misery. It was a road she just wasn't prepared to walk down.

She sat for another five minutes in the quiet room, listening to Melody's steady regular breathing and watching the peaceful baby face. Lucas's bear was tucked under her daughter's arm and the toy confirmed every fear she had, somehow. This had to end, now, tonight. Never mind it had never really started.

Her step was purposeful as she walked downstairs and she had the words trembling on her tongue as she opened the sitting room door.

Lucas was lying slumped on her two-seater sofa, one arm dangling on the floor by his empty plate and the other flung across the cushions in unconscious abandonment. He was fast asleep. Kim stopped just inside the room, her stance like that of a doe before a hunter, and then walked carefully to his side.

Now those riveting eyes were closed and his face was in repose she could see just how exhausted he was. She stared down at him, her eyes drinking in every line and contour of the hard male face. The authoritative sweep of his black brows, the uncompromising cheekbones and determined mouth all spoke of power and hard virility.

It was a face that told the onlooker that subjugation was not an option, that defeat was an unknown and unacceptable concept, and the big lean body and muscled strength evident in every inch of the honed frame was daunting. And sexy. Indescribably sexy.

He was dead to the world. A little shiver ran down her spine and she ached to put her lips against the sleeping

mouth, to trace the faint indentation in the stubbly masculine chin. She should wake him up and tell him to go,
especially in view of what had occurred before she'd gone
upstairs to Melody. He might look curiously vulnerable and
exposed at this moment, but it was an illusion. There wasn't
a vulnerable bone in Lucas's body.

Her eyes lowered to the strong male throat and the be-
ginnings of dark body hair just visible below his open collar, to powerful masculine thighs against which the material
of his trousers were straining.

Was he hairy all over? Her breath caught in her throat
and she suddenly felt as guilty as if she were a peeping
Tom, but she still couldn't seem to tear her eyes away from
the sleeping giant in front of her.

What would it be like to wake up beside him in the
morning after a night of making love? She found she had
no defence against the erotic thoughts crowding her mind.
To taste him, please him, to have him taste and please her?
But she was talking about a lover, here, about giving someone the rights to her body and her life.

Suddenly all the horror connected with the days of her
marriage flooded in and she felt smothered with the weight
of the memories. She took several long deep breaths, pulling at the air as though she were drowning, but still the
feeling of being trapped and desperately frightened was
overwhelming.

She couldn't talk to Lucas now, not now. She needed
time to come to terms with what her head was telling her.
She stood for a moment more and then crept out of the
room to fetch the spare quilt, draping it over the sleeping
form when she returned to the sitting room and turning off
the lights before she closed the door again.

Once in the sanctuary of her bedroom Kim sat on the
edge of the bed and stared vacantly into space.

Lucas Kane was stretched out on her sofa and it looked

as though he was there until morning. She shook her head bewilderedly. Somehow the impossible, the unimaginable had happened. Maggie just wouldn't believe this!

She got ready for bed with both ears straining for the slightest sound from the sitting room, but there was nothing.

Once in bed Kim tried to read for a while but although she dutifully turned the pages she couldn't remember a word she'd read when she thought about it.

Eleven o'clock came and went, then half-past, and finally it was midnight. Lucas was definitely here for the night. Kim put down the book, drank a glass of water and slid down under the covers with a sudden feeling of *que sera sera*.

Short of marching downstairs and throwing him out she could do nothing, she told herself silently, so she might as well try and get some sleep herself. It had been a long day, and an even longer evening, and she had the feeling the next day wasn't going to be any better.

CHAPTER EIGHT

WHEN Kim awoke to the smell of frying bacon she thought for a moment she was still dreaming.

It had been almost light before she had fallen into a fitful doze followed by an hour or two of deep, exhausted slumber, and now, as she glanced at her tiny alarm clock, she saw she had overslept by nearly an hour.

In all the confusion and heart searching of the night before she must have forgotten to set her alarm, she thought feverishly, flinging back the covers as she swung her feet to the floor.

It was unfortunate that Lucas chose that precise moment to enter with a cup of tea. Unfortunate for Kim that was. For Lucas the sight of Kim in a sheer, whisper-thin nightie with her blonde hair tousled and tumbled and her eyes wide with shock was the best start to a day he could remember for a long time.

'Lucas!' Kim shot back in the bed and pulled the covers up to her chin, but not before she had seen the spark of something hot in the silvery eyes.

'I should hope so,' he said calmly. 'Who else were you expecting?'

'I wasn't *expecting* you,' she reminded him severely, her colour high. 'And I'm late; I forgot to set my alarm.'

'Relax.' He strolled over to the bed and her hormones went into hyperdrive. The designer stubble was dynamite. 'You've plenty of time to get Melody to school—and if you're late for work the boss will understand.'

Kim slid a tentative arm from under the covers, the other

still holding the duvet tight round her neck, and took the cup of tea he was offering with a nod of thanks.

'One sugar, I understand?' Lucas said lazily. 'Melody's helping me cook breakfast and is a mine of information as to your likes and dislikes. That's a very intelligent little daughter you've got there.'

'I know.' Just go. *Go*.

'You look gorgeous to wake up to.' Lucas seemed in no hurry to leave, his eyes stroking over her flushed face and his stern mouth uncharacteristically tender.

'You didn't wake up to me,' Kim protested quickly.

'I've recently woken up, you're here...' His words faded as his mouth covered her own and the teacup wobbled alarmingly. The kiss was brief and incredibly sweet, and he studied her face for a moment when he straightened again. 'Gorgeous,' he said softly.

'Lucas, you shouldn't be in here. Melody will think—'

'Absolutely nothing,' he finished for her smoothly. 'There's always a dozen or so small people running about when my family gets together, so I know how children's minds work at Melody's age.'

So that was why he was so comfortable around young children. Kim stared at him, realising—with a touch of exasperation—that everything she learnt about him dispelled the image of a hard-hitting automaton a little more. She wanted to find out he was mean to old ladies, that he didn't like children, that he kicked the cat and beat the dog—anything!

'Do you like children?' It was out before she had time to think.

He didn't seem to consider the question strange. 'When they're like the ones in my family, or Melody,' he said calmly. 'Brats I can do without.' And then he smiled mockingly. 'Not what you wanted to hear?'

'I don't know what you mean.' The colour which had

just begun to diminish returned in a fresh surge of scarlet. Impossible man!

'Of course you don't,' he taunted softly.

She wasn't going to win this one. Kim tried to look stern and assertive. 'Where's Melody?' she asked pointedly.

'Sitting at the breakfast bar, eating a bowl of Frosties,' Lucas returned easily, 'before her bacon and egg. Speaking of which—' he dropped another kiss on her nose before turning and walking out of the room, saying over his shoulder '—you can be first in the shower but you'd better be quick. Breakfast will be ready in five minutes.'

First in the shower, for goodness' sake! As the door closed behind Lucas's big frame, Kim found herself glaring across the room. Anyone would think he lived here the way he was carrying on.

And then, before she had time to school her features into anything resembling sweetness, the door opened again and Lucas popped his head round. 'I forgot to say thanks for the bed and board,' he said softly, his eyes amused as they took in her expression. 'I appreciate it more than I can say, Kim.'

She managed a creditably gracious smile. 'That's okay; you were obviously out on your feet. I'd have done the same for anybody.'

'Now don't spoil it. And you're down to four minutes, thirty seconds, by the way.'

Kim had time to do no more than shower and slip into her bathrobe before breakfast, piling her hair into a towel turban-style before running downstairs to the kitchen.

Lucas and Melody were perched on the two high stools the small kitchen boasted in front of the minuscule breakfast bar, and they looked comfortable together. Too comfortable. Melody was in the middle of one of her long and involved stories about a happening at school to which Lucas was giving his full attention, and as Kim surveyed

Melody's animated face and Lucas's patient one she felt a dart of pure panic.

'Mummy!' Melody saw her first. 'Lucas has cooked bacon and eggs and he says I can have mine in a bun. Can I, Mummy?'

'If you eat it all up,' said Kim mechanically, walking across and kissing the top of Melody's fair head as Lucas slid off his stool and waved for her to be seated.

They ate with Lucas propping up the sink unit as he devoured three buns bursting with bacon and egg whilst Melody looked on with unconcealed admiration.

Her daughter clearly thought he was the best thing since sliced bread, Kim told herself crossly, and Lucas was playing up to his role of man of the hour with gusto. Immediately as the thought hit she acknowledged its unfairness. Lucas was just being Lucas, she admitted miserably, which made everything a thousand times worse and a million times more dangerous.

'Can I ask a favour?'

As Melody danced off upstairs to change from her pyjamas into her school clothes Lucas perched himself on the stool she had vacated. It brought him close, much, much too close, and Kim's voice was something of a snap as she said, 'Yes?'

'Do you have a razor I can use?'

It wasn't what she had expected and of course he knew that only too well, Kim thought nastily, but although she knew she was blushing she kept her voice very even when she said, 'I've only light duty disposables that I use for my legs, I'm afraid. I'm not sure they'll cope with a man's beard.'

'I'll manage.'

And then, before she was aware of what he was doing, he had moved his stool in front of hers so that his long legs were either side of her.

'You've a crumb on your chin.' His voice was soft as
he reached out and stroked her skin, and she felt terribly
aware that she only had her bra and panties on beneath her
towelling robe.

She knew what he wanted—it was written all over his
dark face—but the shiver that slithered down her spine was
more of anticipation than apprehension as his mouth lowered to hers and his whole body seemed to enclose her.

He kissed her slowly and thoroughly, taking his time,
savouring her lips with a pleasure that was visible. His
tongue nuzzled her teeth and as her mouth opened to ac-
commodate him he plunged immediately into the secret ter-
ritory, fuelling her desire with a heady rush of sensation
that made her gasp out loud.

When he pulled her off the stool to stand in front of him
she was powerless to resist, even when his hands slid beneath the folds of the robe to the warm silky flesh beneath.
His fingers were possessively skilful as he brought her
breasts to tingling life through the lace of her bra, and the
sharp little needles of pleasure grew and grew in time with
her pounding heartbeat.

His thighs were hard against hers, the image of his sex-
uality stamped forcefully on her soft belly, and Kim could
feel his heart slamming against his ribcage like a sledge-
hammer as he allowed the kiss to deepen into an intimate
assault on her senses that was almost like a consummation
in itself.

And then, slowly, she felt the embrace change, his hands
continuing to stroke and pet her as they moved to the small
of her back but with a control that restrained even as it
pleasured.

She raised dazed eyes to his and the silver gaze was
waiting for her, his voice rough and not quite steady as he
said, 'Melody is upstairs,' and then, when he could see she
was still too bemused and disorientated to understand,

'Another minute and I wouldn't be able to stop. Okay? You do something to me, Kim. Something mind-blowing.'

'Do I?' she asked faintly, aware the towel had fallen as her hair tumbled free.

She raised a trembling hand to push back the heavy fall of silk from her face as she spoke, and as she flung back the shining, thick curtain the robe fell fully open, revealing her slender, honey-tinted, rounded curves to Lucas's hungry eyes.

With a wordless exclamation Lucas pulled her to his chest again and kissed her hard on the lips, his mouth urgent and expressing the desire that still had Kim weak and shaky. 'It'd be good between us—you know that, don't you?' he whispered huskily. 'Say it, tell me you know it too.'

Yes, it would be good, incredible, but what about when it ended? Kim asked herself silently. How did one cope in the aftermath of a nuclear missile exploding everything that was safe and familiar to smithereens?

She had never wanted this. She had never wanted to fall in love again. And then she froze, her face turning as white as a sheet as the truth she had been trying to fight for weeks refused to be ignored any longer. She loved Lucas. She *loved* him.

'Kim?' He had been watching her closely and his voice was terse. 'What's the matter?'

'Nothing.' All the desire and excitement his love-making had induced was gone and she felt as cold as ice.

'You look like someone has just kicked you in the teeth so don't tell me nothing,' Lucas said as evenly as he could, struggling for calmness.

'I said nothing is the matter, so nothing is the matter,' she said numbly, struggling out of his arms with a strength that took him by surprise. 'Just leave me alone, Lucas.'

'Leave you alone?' he said incredulously.

'Yes.' She was crying and screaming inside but her voice was actually cool, she thought amazedly. 'I want you to leave, *now.*'

'Oh, no—oh, no, sugar.' There was a raw determination in his voice that was even stronger than the anger. 'No way. We've come a long way since October and I'm sure as hell not going backwards. You talk to me.'

'You can't make me do anything.' Her chin was sticking right out but the fear and defiance in her face was all at odds with what he was asking. Lucas stared at her, recognising that this opposition had its roots in something much more deep than their conversation that morning. And, for all her aggression, she looked about as old as Melody right at this moment.

His anger collapsed. 'No, you're right,' he said quietly, 'but only because I don't and wouldn't operate like that. Brute force or any sort of blackmail is not my style, Kim. But nevertheless we *are* going to talk. And do you know why?'

She stared at him, her eyes wide and enormous in the lint paleness of her face.

'Because I love you,' he said softly.

'No!' It brought a response but not the one he had hoped for. Lucas felt as though ice-cold water had been thrown at him but he didn't betray it by the flicker of an eyelash.

'Yes,' he said coolly. 'I've been around enough to know the real thing when it happens, Kim. And just for the record I've never said that to another woman, not even in the most…intimate times.'

She jerked her head, her eyes wild as she went for the jugular in an effort to make him leave. 'And there have been plenty of those,' she flung at him tightly.

'I've not been celibate,' he agreed with silky smoothness, 'but licentiousness has never held any appeal.'

'I don't want a relationship with you.' She said it slowly,

with a sharp little pause in between each word, and Lucas felt his anger mounting again at the sheer intractability in her face.

'Then you'll spell out why,' he ground out equally slowly. 'You owe me that at least and I'm not budging until we have that talk, Kim. Take Melody to school and then come back here. I mean it.'

She had heard that particular note in his voice too many times over the last months to doubt it, normally when he was digging his heels in over a business situation that seemed impossible and which he was determined to change. But he couldn't change her. Not now, not ever. But she would talk to him. Perhaps when he heard it all he would realise she was serious? And she was. Oh, she was, she told herself desperately. But how was she going to tell him about the humiliations, the awfulness of it all? But she'd have to; it was the only way.

'All right.' It was dull, lifeless, and took away any triumph Lucas might have felt.

Melody was all skips and smiles and giggles when Kim came downstairs from getting dressed a little later, and once her daughter had said goodbye to Lucas—insisting on being lifted up into his arms so she could kiss his cheek—she gambolled out to the car like a spring lamb.

The reason for her exuberance became apparent once they were on their way to school.

'Is Lucas going to be my new daddy?' Melody asked interestedly, almost causing Kim to swerve into the kerb.

'What?' Her voice was too shrill and she tried to moderate it a little as she said, 'What do you mean, sweetheart? Of course not.'

'Aw.' Melody grimaced at her like a dissatisfied elf. 'Susan has got a new daddy and so has Kerry, and Kerry's daddy makes her breakfast. She told me. And he brings her presents sometimes.'

The penny dropped. Kim took a long silent breath as she searched for the right words and then said carefully, 'People often bring other people presents, chicken, just to be nice, especially grown-ups for children.'

'And do people stay and cook breakfast too?'

'Sometimes.'

'I *like* Lucas.' It was defiant and hopeful and bewildered all in one, and Kim's heart went out to the small scrap of humanity at the side of her.

'And he likes you too, darling,' she assured Melody quickly.

'But not enough to be my new daddy?'

This child of her heart had a way of going straight for the kernel in the nut. Kim glanced at her helplessly. 'There's more to being a daddy than that,' she managed softly. 'Adult things, and very complicated. But Lucas likes you every bit as much as you like him, I promise you.'

She could feel Melody gazing at her and prepared herself for what might come next, but in the mercurial way of children Melody suddenly tired of that avenue of thought and said instead, 'I got all my letters right yesterday, Mummy. Even the hard ones.'

'Well done, darling.'

'Kerry didn't. And she can't hop, either.'

So a new daddy didn't provide the answer to everything. Kim's hand reached out and squeezed one of Melody's for a moment. They would get through this. Somehow.

On the way back to the house Kim found she was shaking, and she stopped the car in a quiet lay-by for a few minutes to give herself the chance to calm down and prepare for what lay ahead.

Somehow, and she still wasn't quite sure how or when the situation had escalated so alarmingly, she was going to have to convince Lucas she wasn't in the market for an affair, albeit a potentially serious one from his comment about loving her. Did he? Did he love her? Kim considered the possibility with tightly shut eyes, her hands resting limply on the steering wheel.

How could you want something and yet fear it so much it made you nauseous at the same time? she asked herself silently, dragging in the air through lips that trembled.

Love meant disappointment and betrayal and bitter hurt. She knew that; she *knew* it. It meant a transference of power from one person to another with terrifying consequences. It meant subjugation and a bondage that was worse than anything in the physical realm because it involved the heart, the emotions, the very essence of who you were.

She couldn't really remember her parents beyond a deep male voice mixed with the faint odour of cigar smoke, and the feel of her mother's softness enveloping her in a warm, secure, satisfying embrace in the middle of the night when—presumably—she had woken from some bad dream or other. But she could remember her Aunt Mabel. Remember the promises that she was safe now, that everything would be all right, that she would be loved and looked after like Mummy and Daddy would have wanted.

And then her aunt had gone, and she had found herself in an alien environment. She had cried and screamed, she could recall that as though it were yesterday, and someone—a trained child counsellor, probably—had explained everything to her.

It hadn't been until much later that she had realised her Aunt Mabel, who for two years had been her security and base, hadn't made any provision for her. Had left her at the mercy of those relatives who had descended like vultures on her aunt's estate.

Kim opened her eyes wide and stared straight ahead. And then there had been Graham... Her face set in rigid control and she turned the ignition key with a sharp movement of her hand.

Lucas was waiting for her when she drew up outside the cottage. He looked tough, remote, but she now knew that remoteness of his was a devastating weapon which he used with expert finesse, lulling one into a false security that was deadly.

'The coffee's ready.' His voice was gentle—deliberately so, Kim warned herself silently.

'Lucas, this is pointless, us talking like this,' Kim nerved herself to say quickly.

'I disagree.' He smiled blandly.

Kim tried a different approach. 'The Marsden contract is hanging on a thread,' she reminded him evenly. 'You were supposed to call Miles Marsden at nine this morning.'

Lucas suggested somewhere that Miles Marsden could go before narrowing his eyes and staring at her fixedly. She stared back for a moment before the silver gaze became unbearable.

'Coffee,' he reaffirmed smoothly, his voice firm but expressionless. 'I've got used to my daily quota and I can't do without it, or perhaps I should say I don't intend to do without it.'

They weren't talking about coffee. Kim walked past him into the hall as he waved her over the threshold of the house, and again she had the feeling that she was the guest and Lucas the host. It rankled but she welcomed the shot of adrenalin; she would take any Dutch courage she could get to see her through the next little while.

Kim continued through to the kitchen and she saw immediately that Lucas had restored the place to its usual gleaming brightness. The only hint of their earlier breakfast was the faint smell of bacon.

'You shouldn't have cleared up,' she said stiffly. 'There was no need.'

He ignored the comment as though she hadn't spoken, following her into the limited space and leaning against the wall, his hands thrust deep into his trouser pockets and his eyes broodingly intent.

He had shaved whilst she'd been gone. Kim found her gaze drawn to the hard square jaw and her heart gave a little kick. And showered too by the look of his still-damp hair.

Kim found she was moving jerkily as she poured the two cups of coffee; the liquid steel gaze was far too intense to be comfortable. She swallowed hard as she handed Lucas his coffee, keeping her gaze fixed on a spot over his left shoulder.

'Thanks.' He straightened as he took the cup and she felt her senses respond with humiliating swiftness. 'So...' He made no effort to stand aside and unless she literally barged past him she was effectively trapped in her little part of the kitchen. 'I told you I loved you and you reacted by telling me to get the hell out. Care to explain why?' he asked with a cool lack of expression.

'Would you listen if I said no, I wouldn't?' Kim responded painfully.

'No.'

'I thought not.'

Where could she start? She took a hefty gulp of the scalding hot coffee and then winced as it burnt her throat, her eyes smarting. 'Do you want me to resign?' she asked quietly, knowing she was prevaricating.

'No, Kim, I do not want you to resign,' Lucas said with formidable control. 'I want you to talk to me.'

He was asking for the hardest thing in the world, as though it was as easy as falling off a log. She stared at him, her face tight with tension, and then looked down into the rich warmth of the fragrant coffee as she said very softly, 'It's a long story and it won't change anything.'

'I'll be the judge of that.'

She looked up at him then, searching her mind for an

escape route, but there wasn't one. She had known all along there wouldn't be. He had made up his mind he wanted the 't's crossed and the 'i's dotted and, Lucas being Lucas, that was exactly what he would get. Never mind about her pain, her humiliation, her excruciating shame...

She took a deep breath and began talking. It wasn't so bad at first; she began with the agony of her aunt dying and the way she had been whisked into care, detailing the fight to rise above the loneliness and isolation she had felt in a steady quiet voice. And then she paused, her voice very low as she said, 'And then I went to university and met Graham.'

'Did you love him?' Lucas asked softly.

'I thought I did.' She smiled bitterly. 'It was so amazing to have someone need me so badly, to want to be with me every minute, to love me so much. I'd never had that before and it quite literally bowled me off my feet. *Graham* bowled me off my feet. And then we got married.' She stopped abruptly, feeling horribly trapped and moving restlessly in the tiny space. 'Can we go through to the sitting room?'

'Sure.' He gently touched her cheek with one large hand before standing aside to let her pass. His fingers were cool, steady, and the tingling sensation in her flesh made her suddenly short of breath. It made her scurry through to the sitting room with more haste than dignity, and as she turned to face him again he raised his eyebrows at her.

'I wasn't going to ravish you on the kitchen floor.'

'I know that.'

'You don't lie very well, Kim,' said Lucas matter-of-factly. 'Continue with the story. You're now married.'

It sounded simple when it was said like that.

'Graham didn't love me,' Kim said mechanically, forcing herself to go into automatic to get through the next minutes. 'I don't actually think he was capable of the emotion. He'd put on a good show at university and we always seemed to be with a load of people there, the life was so gregarious. His drinking didn't stand out there, either; everyone in Graham's set drank too much.'

Lucas nodded. 'I too was young once,' he said drily.

'His parents financed a little business for him and he was pleased with that at first, acting the big I am among his friends and cronies. But the drinking was getting worse. I tried to help him but he'd turn everything round on me, saying he had to drink because I was a useless wife, hopeless in bed, that sort of thing.'

She had tried to continue in the flat even tone but the pain of Graham's rejection, the incredibly cruel things he had used to throw at her, was still a raw wound.

'We'd been married eighteen months when he suggested...' Kim sat down on one of the easy chairs, her head lowered and her hair covering her face like a veil. She had felt too weary that morning to fiddle with it before taking Melody to school, but she was glad now of the slight protection it gave from those piercing eyes.

'What did he suggest, Kim?' Lucas said tensely.

'He asked...he wanted me to sleep with one of his prospective clients,' Kim said numbly. 'He'd been furious when I got pregnant with Melody so quickly after we'd got married, and when I wouldn't have an abortion like he wanted he blamed that—the added responsibility of a family—on the business failing. He said I owed him.'

Lucas swore softly but the sound was none the less ugly for its quietness. He knew this slimeball's type; unfortunately there were several spawned in each generation. Men without conscience, men who would use vulnerability and gentleness in another person to bring them under their domination. Kim had been a sitting target for him with her background, and with her looks he must have thought he'd won the jackpot.

'Melody was five months old,' Kim continued quietly, 'and right up to that point I'd tried to convince myself that I could turn the marriage around, for our child's sake if nothing else. I'd done everything I could to make him love me, tried to please him in every way I knew how.' She stopped again, the memory of her abasement from those days horribly vivid. How often, in the weeks and months following Graham's vile request, had she told herself she must have been mad, insane, not to see what he was really like? But she hadn't. She just hadn't.

'But that day I went berserk.' Her voice was shaking now in spite of her efforts to control it. 'Really berserk. I flew at him, hitting him, punching him, and he struck me back so hard I lost consciousness for a time.'

'Hell, Kim.' He knew she probably didn't want to be touched, not in view of what she was reliving, but Lucas couldn't see her sitting there, so small and slender and broken, and not hold her. He lifted her up to him, and as she stiffened, her body tensing, he said softly, 'It's all right, it's all right; I just want to hold you as one human being comforting another, that's all. Nothing more, Kim. I swear it.'

He would have given the world for five minutes alone with Graham Allen if the dirty swine hadn't been dead. And he would have made him suffer. An artery pumping out his life blood had been too quick an end for the so-and-so.

'When I came to he was sitting in front of me with Melody on his knee,' Kim whispered against his shirt, her head still hanging limply. 'He told me if I ever confided in a living soul, told them anything of what had gone on, he would kill her, and then me. I believed him, Lucas. He was actually capable of that when the mood took him. He said it was important for the business he was seen as an established family man and that if I tried to leave him he would find us. He did promise he'd never hit me again, though.'

'You should have left him. There are places—'

'No. He'd have found us.' Kim raised desolate eyes, her lashes starred with tears. 'But from that day I moved into Melody's room on a camp bed. I couldn't bear for him to touch me. Something died for ever that day, Lucas. I know it. I could never trust any man again.'

'I'm not any man,' he said grimly, seating himself on the sofa with Kim on his knee and holding her when she would have struggled away.

'Things got worse and worse,' Kim continued, her body tight and rigid. 'He…he became like a devil. And then, the night after the shopping incident, when he'd broken his word and hit me again, he found me looking at flats in the paper. He attacked me, said I was withholding his conjugal rights so he'd take what was rightfully his by force if he had to. But I fought back, hit him over the head with a saucepan in the end and locked myself in Melody's room. I thought he might try to break the door down but in the event he went off on a drinking binge, and the rest you know.'

She took a deep breath. 'Except that he left debts, huge debts—for me, that is—and I was stupid enough to have signed documents that made me as responsible as Graham.'

'Hence you jumping at the job at Kane Electrical,' Lucas said softly, his voice shaking a little with what he was feeling. 'And here was me thinking you had fallen for my irresistible charm.'

He was trying to lighten things, Kim knew that, but his closeness was too much to cope with. 'Please let me go, Lucas,' she said tremblingly. 'And don't feel sorry for me. I didn't tell you about Graham for that.'

'Listen to me, Kim.' He lifted her chin so that she had to look into his face, and she saw fierce anger was battling with a tenderness that made her want to howl like a baby. 'I can't deny I want him to suffer the torments of the damned for what he's put you through, and if he were alive I'd find him and teach him a lesson that would mark him until his dying day. That's the way I'm made, I'm afraid. But you've got to put that maniac behind you. He's history, dead, gone—and I don't mean in just the physical sense.'

She was dazed and shaking, as much by their intimacy as the terror she had relived.

'If you let him shape your future he's really won, don't you see that?' Lucas urged huskily. 'And you're worth more than the dregs he's left you, and so is Melody.'

'Melody is one reason I don't want a relationship with anyone, ever,' Kim said tightly, afraid the pull of his magnetism was going to convince her black was white. 'We're safe as we are, Melody and I, and that's all I ask of the future, Lucas. To be safe.'

'The hell it is.' It was a growl, and immediately he added, 'I'm sorry. Don't look like that; I'm not going to hurt you, for crying out loud. But, like I said before, I'm not anyone, and what's between us is something outside the normal realm of things. Of course you want to be safe, but there's more to life than just that, my love. Don't throw all your hopes and dreams and aspirations on the funeral pyre of that rat. I can make you alive in a way you've never dreamt of.'

My love. Kim couldn't speak at all, she could only look at him, but her eyes were huge with distrust and fear and he read the panic and denial in her face with deep and silent frustration.

'I want you, Kim, but not for a night or a week or a month,' he said very softly.

'No.' Before he could say any more she jerked herself away from him, sliding to her feet and shaking uncontrollably as she said, 'You have to understand, Lucas, please. I can't… I don't want commitment.'

How many times had he said exactly that to some beauty or other he was inviting into his bed? Lucas's thoughts were self-derisory and caustic. And now he was being hoist with his own petard. But he was damned if he was going to let her go. She was his, in her heart. He just had to convince her of it. But she had had enough brute force and manipulation to last her a lifetime and he wasn't about to indulge in more of the same. If he took her she would capitulate in seconds; he had no doubt about that. But he wanted more than her body and a momentary acceptance in her emotions. Much more.

'Okay.' He stood up slowly to face her, thrusting his hands into his pockets to remind himself not to touch her. How he wanted to touch her…

'Okay?' The tears were still sparkling on her white cheeks and Kim took a shaky breath. 'What do you mean okay?'

'I accept your proviso that we're just friends,' Lucas said evenly, 'and I appreciate that you trusted me enough to tell me about your past. That's the first requisite of friends, trust.'

Kim stared at him, feeling she was entering an Alice in Wonderland experience. She hadn't mentioned anything about being friends, had she? she asked herself bewilderedly. And where had he got this idea about her trusting him?

'So, we'll go on from here with no bad blood between us, yes?' Lucas's tone was soothing. He had noted the brittle stance of her body, her chalk-white face and agonised eyes, and it had warned him she was at the limit of her endurance for one day. He also knew he wanted her more than ever.

'I…I don't know,' Kim stammered defensively, suddenly unsure of exactly what was being said.

'Kim, you've told me you need to work to pay off Graham's debts,' Lucas said calmly, 'and surely you want to provide Melody with the best standard of living in the meantime? That taken as read, you working as my secretary is a good deal for both of us. I get someone who is completely trustworthy and willing to give the job her all; you get an excellent salary with no strings attached.'

'But…but what you said…'

'About loving you, wanting you?' Lucas expelled a quite breath. 'That still stands, I'm afraid, but I'm no callow youth in the grip of adolescent urgings he can't control. And life goes on, even in the midst of my bruised ego. I'm a businessman first and foremost, Kim. You should know everything comes second to that.' And the funny thing was, he would have meant that last sentence at one time, Lucas admitted with bitter self-mockery.

'The last few months have been somewhat…strained at times, haven't they?' Lucas raised dark sardonic eyebrows, and at Kim's faint nod inclined his own head in agreement. 'But now we both know exactly where we stand and with no hard feelings. Okay?'

'Okay.'

He smiled as she spoke but Kim was beyond smiling back. Her eyes opened wide as he placed his hands on her slender shoulders but she stood quietly before him, forcing herself not to shrink away. And when the dark head bent and he lightly brushed the top of her head with his lips she still remained motionless, wondering—with a bewilderment that was stronger than anything she'd felt before—why she felt her heart was breaking.

CHAPTER NINE

KIM didn't go into work that day although Lucas left immediately after their 'clearing of the air', as he referred to their talk.

He had ordered her to go back to bed and get some sleep before she had to collect Melody again, but she found sleep was the last thing on her mind in the hours that followed. After an hour or so of tossing and turning she threw back the covers irritably and got dressed again, giving the house an impromptu spring-clean that took all the rest of the day and most of the evening.

The hard physical work helped; at least she fell asleep as soon as her head touched the pillow that night, and her dreams—if she had any—must have been non-threatening because she couldn't remember them in the morning, which was a Saturday.

She found her heart was beating so hard it was suffocating the first time she met Lucas after the morning at the cottage, but he had retreated into the hard, attractive, distant tycoon of earlier days and within an hour or two—amazingly to Kim—she found herself relaxing, and by the end of Monday she was sufficiently loosened up to laugh at one of his wickedly amusing observations on life.

The next morning she experienced the same hot shivers and thudding of the heart as the day before, but when Lucas made no attempt to be close or anything but her boss, their old working relationship gradually settled into place.

The silver-grey eyes still pinned her on occasion but that was Lucas, she assured herself each time she caught him looking at her in a certain way. And the habit he had of almost reading her mind was peculiar to him too. It didn't make her comfortable, but cosiness or serenity had never been an option around Lucas anyway.

Kim found she was missing Maggie more than she would have thought possible as the days and weeks crept by, especially after one of her friend's phone calls or letters which were all determinedly cheerful and which never mentioned Pete.

She had mentioned Maggie's situation to Lucas whilst assuring him she would make alternative arrangements for Melody, should the need arise, but it was four weeks before this happened and then the late meeting just necessitated Janie—the mother of Melody's schoolfriend—walking across the road to the school and keeping Melody until seven, when Kim collected her.

By the time the May blossom had fallen and June had arrived, and Melody was well underway with her herb and vegetable patch, Kim was forced to acknowledge to herself that she was lonely. She adored Melody, worshipped her, but the lack of adult stimulation was getting to her, she told herself crossly one Saturday morning after a particularly vivid and erotic dream concerning Lucas.

She missed Maggie's easy, funny companionship, that was all it was. She narrowed her eyes against the hot June sunlight streaming in through the kitchen window. But it wasn't, was it? her innate honesty forced her to recognise in the next moment.

It wasn't so much that she was lonely as lonely for Lucas, and there was a subtle difference there. Since she had accepted that she loved him there was barely a minute or two that ticked by that he wasn't on her mind. It wasn't so bad when she was at work—at least she could see him there, hear him talk, laugh at his jokes and exist on the perimeter of his busy life.

Sad girl. The thought was immediate and extremely annoying, but truthful. She hunched her shoulders against it and frowned at the sunlight.

And all the long work lunches they shared didn't help. She was forced to see him in a different light when he took her to one of the little restaurants he favoured, or to the pub, and although he assured her he'd treated June exactly the same and it was the way he liked to relate to his secretaries, it nevertheless caused Kim untold painful heartsearchings.

As had the couple of times she had found herself at his home. She'd met Martha, his housekeeper, and the animal occupants of the beautiful mansion. Again, good reasons for her being there—the first time he had called in on his way back to the office after lunch for a file he'd forgotten, and the next he had asked her to bring some papers to him one morning when he had been working at home, but each time Martha had insisted Kim partake of coffee and homemade shortbread before she had left, and treated her as—what, exactly? Kim asked herself silently. A buddy, a friend? Certainly not as one of Lucas's employees.

And Lucas's relationship with his housekeeper she'd found particularly unsettling. His gentle teasing of the little old grey-haired woman, the warmth and tenderness in Lucas's voice, and the blatant devotion in Martha's when she spoke of the man she called 'my wee lad' had all been disconcerting. Unnerving even.

Not that Lucas had stepped out of line for a minute. Oh, no, not ice-man. 'Oh, stop it.' Kim acknowledged she was being spectacularly unfair. It was just that she hadn't expected her 'just friends' decision to be quite so hard, or so apparently easy for him! Sour grapes. Kim nodded to the accusation. Probably. Which made her really mean.

Enough. Get your mind off Lucas and on to something else, she told herself sternly, and with that in mind she walked out of the kitchen door into the spangled sunlight of the garden. 'Fancy the paddling pool out, sweetheart?' she called to Melody, who was busily engaged in looking for weeds in her little plot of ground.

A whoop of delight was the answer, and within half an hour the paddling pool was full and they were both in their bikinis, Melody splashing about in the tepid water and Kim sitting in a deckchair under the shade of a copper beech with a mug of coffee in her hand.

An abundance of wisteria had gracefully draped itself over the adjoining garden wall during May, and this was now giving way to a cascade of rambling roses, their delicious scent wafting gently on the still air.

It was a world away from the nightmare of the little bedsit they had endured for two long years. Hot tears pricked at Kim's eyes—which was ridiculous, she told herself firmly, when she ought to be smiling if anything. But Lucas had made all this possible—given her back her independence, her chance of carving a good life for herself and Melody, of living somewhere like this. And she was grateful, incredibly so, but she'd never really told him.

She blinked very hard. And sooner or later some woman, a little more beautiful or talented or charismatic than the rest, would snare him. She wasn't aware he was dating again but he could be, for all she knew, and she couldn't blame him if he was. As he'd said, celibacy wasn't his style.

And it would be her fault. Her fault she had missed a chance of heaven. But... Kim stared straight ahead but the garden had vanished into the black abyss of her thoughts. If she had her chance over again she would do exactly the same. She might be throwing away her chance of heaven but the hell she had endured with Graham precluded stepping into a relationship again. With Graham she'd had the excuse she hadn't known what she was doing, but there would be no justification for willingly putting herself and Melody at risk again.

The same old arguments and counter-arguments she had mentally indulged in for the last two months raged in her mind, and when Melody tapped her arm impatiently, saying, 'Mummy, *Mummy*. I said I can hear the doorbell,' it took Kim a few seconds to bring herself back to the real world.

'I'm sorry, sweetheart. Mummy was daydreaming.' Kim smiled into the little face frowning up at her, hastily reaching for the cloudy blue sarong that matched the bikini as she rose.

She wrapped the delicately patterned cloth round her waist as she entered the house and padded through the hall to the front door, and it was only as she opened it she realised she hadn't given a thought to who might be calling at ten o'clock on a sunny June morning.

'Lucas!' For a moment she stared blankly at the tall, lean figure in front of her dressed casually in a charcoal shirt and black jeans, but as the silver eyes narrowed slightly and showed their appreciation of her clothes—or lack of them—reality surged in in an overwhelmingly hot flood that started at her toes and worked upwards.

Kim resisted the impulse to cross her arms over her breasts and said instead, her voice as cool as she could make it, considering she was giving a first-rate impression of a furnace at full tilt, 'What's the matter? Is anything wrong?'

'Plenty,' he drawled lazily, 'the first thing being that I'm kicking myself for not calling round before, this summer.'

She tried for a smile, which was a mistake because it turned into more of a nervous twitch, and then, as she heard Melody's excited voice just behind her calling Lucas's name, Kim groaned inwardly. If she knew anything about her hospitable little daughter, Lucas was going to be invited to come and see Melody's new paddling pool, which of course was fine, great—or would have been if her mother wasn't half-naked!

'Lucas!' Melody skidded along the hall on small bare wet feet and with an abandonment Kim envied, and as Lucas bent down and held out his arms Melody jumped right into them. 'I kept asking Mummy when you'd come and she said she didn't know,' Melody told him as she put small hands on his shoulders and looked into the dark rugged face. 'She said you were busy.'

'Not too busy to call and see you,' Lucas said easily, straightening with Melody still perched in his arms and standing to look at Kim. Two pairs of eyes, one glittering metallic silver and the other deep liquid brown, surveyed her unblinkingly, and Kim sighed her acquiescence to the unspoken request.

'You'd better come in,' she said a touch ungraciously to Lucas. She couldn't fight them both.

'Thank you,' he said with mocking gratefulness, and the colour which had just begun to die down returned with new ferocity.

Irritating, impossible man! All the warmer feelings she'd indulged in earlier went right out of the window.

'Coffee?' She led the way down the hall, painfully aware of the transparency of the sarong and the revealing nature of the bikini. The purchase of the bikini had been in the nature of a statement one Saturday a few weeks before.

Lucas had taken her out to lunch the previous day, and as they'd been leaving the restaurant there had been a low and discreet call from a table across the room, and a woman had made her way to their side. An exquisitely dressed and equally exquisitely beautiful woman.

Lucas had introduced them, and Kim had been very conscious of a pair of green feline eyes looking her over from head to toe. Perfectly painted, glossy lips had managed a half-smile before the woman had gone on to ask if Lucas was coming to some party or other that weekend. 'It will be such fun, darling,' the carefully modulated voice had urged seductively. 'Clarice's little get-togethers always are. Remember the last time when we finished up in the pool and I lost my bikini top? A designer one, too, darling,' she added in an aside to Kim. 'Although Lucas found it for me.'

She just bet Lucas had. Kim's face must have spoken volumes because she remembered Lucas's mockingly cynical smile as he had made their goodbyes, and led her out of the restaurant with a light hand at her elbow.

'An old friend?' She'd resisted asking until they were nearly back at the office.

Lucas had shrugged easily. 'In a manner of speaking.'

'The party sounded as though it was a bit wild,' Kim had said brightly, hating him.

'Not really.' Amused eyes had rested on her flushed face for a moment. 'Felicity could make a wake sound like a riot. Clarice and her husband recently spent a fortune on an indoor pool that could house the Olympics, so now every invitation comes in an evening dress and swimwear form. Clarice just likes to be different.'

'Evening dress *and* designer swimwear,' Kim had said tartly. 'The competition must be fierce.'

'I wouldn't know.' They'd arrived back at Kane Electrical and Lucas had driven smoothly into his parking space before turning to her, resting his arm casually on the back of her seat. 'I prefer *au naturel*, myself, but if I have to wear something a pair of old jeans will do.'

The mental pictures that had flashed on to the screen of her mind had taken some working through, but by the time Kim had left the building later that day she'd managed to get her errant thoughts under control. Just.

However, the image of a green-eyed, red-haired beauty

had stayed with her, along with the uncomfortable knowledge that the only item of swimwear *she* possessed was a very functional one-piece that had seen better days. She had bought the bikini and matching sarong the next day.

'If you go out into the garden with Melody I'll bring the coffee in a minute,' Kim offered coolly once they were in the kitchen and Lucas was standing by the open back door.

He looked very dark and masculine in her little limed-oak kitchen and every bit as disturbing as the most erotic of her dreams.

'No hurry.' Melody had nestled herself comfortably in his arms, half-turned so that her fair head was resting against his collarbone and her face was turned towards Kim. 'We're fine.'

He was making no secret of the fact that he was enjoying looking at her, and Kim was distinctly conscious of the briefness of the bikini and the deep V between her tingling breasts. And of Melody next to his heart. The pose was relaxed and Lucas looked natural, like a father. It sent such whirling panic through her she almost dropped the coffee pot.

Once in the garden Lucas refused Kim's offer of the deck-chair and lay sprawled out at her feet after insisting she be seated. It caused her equilibrium untold problems to see his dark head at a level with her thighs, his long, lean muscled body propped on one elbow as he surveyed Melody splashing in the sunlit water.

'A water baby.' His deep voice was lazy and amused and Kim bitterly resented his imperturbability when she hardly knew where to put herself.

'She's always loved the water.' It was tight and stiff but the best she could do. She paused a moment, trying to make her voice normal before she asked, 'Why are you here, Lucas?'

'Because it's a beautiful day, Maggie is in America and

I thought you might be able to use a friend's company,' he said quietly, still with his gaze directed at the small figure in front of them.

He'd done it again, read her mind. Kim didn't know whether to be angry or thrilled, but in view of all the complications that went hand in hand with this man she decided on the former.

'That's very kind of you,' she began tersely, 'but—'

'No, it's not kind, Kim.' He looked up at her then, and she felt her breath leave her body at the intensity in the beautiful silver eyes. 'It's selfish, if you really want to know. I want to be here with you, and with Melody. I've wanted to be with you every damn weekend for months and this morning I decided enough was enough.'

'Oh.' She stared at him, totally taken aback and with all coherent thought clean gone.

'So what do you say to a day together?' he asked slowly.

He wasn't touching her, not in any physical way, but Kim could feel the power of his magnetic personality reaching out and enclosing her. He looked hard and dark and sexy, and she found herself beginning to tremble.

'I thought perhaps lunch at a little place I know,' he continued quietly, 'and then an afternoon on the river, followed by dinner at my place. Martha is standing by for Melody's likes and dislikes.'

'Lucas—'

'Just friends, Kim, if that's what you want.' He surveyed her with unfathomable eyes. 'You can't deny you could use a friend right now.'

A friend was one thing; Lucas Kane was quite another. Nevertheless the thought of a day with him was like Christmas and New Year rolled into one and magnified a million times, and Kim felt her resolve wavering. And then Melody took the decision right out of her hands when her daughter came to stand in front of them, small hands on tiny hips, as she said, 'Can Lucas stay for lunch, Mummy? *Please?*'

Kim hesitated for a moment, but it was long enough for Lucas to sense her indecisiveness and capitalise on it with the ruthlessness that was an integral part of him. 'Better than that,' he said lightly. 'We're going out to lunch and then you can have a ride in a boat on the river—would you like that? And if you're *very* good...'

'What? What?' As Lucas let his voice die away mysteriously, Melody jumped up and down in her excitement.

'If you're very good you can come and see where I live,' Lucas said softly, 'and meet Jasper and Sultan.'

'Who are Jasper and Sultan?'

'My dogs—very big dogs.'

'Do they bite?'

'They don't know how to bite,' Lucas assured her seriously, 'only how to lick.'

Melody nodded, believing him utterly. 'I like dogs like that,' she stated firmly.

Kim looked at them helplessly, and then, as Lucas raised his eyes to hers, the crystal gaze pinned her. 'Go and get changed,' he said very quietly, 'while I wait for you.'

They continued looking at each other for a second, and Kim's pulse leapt at the tone of the last words. He was an enigma, this man. Every time she thought she had got him worked out he did something to amaze her, the way he had today. But whereas all Graham's surprises had been nasty ones, everything she learnt about Lucas just made her love him more.

It was too dangerous a line to pursue, and Kim held out her hand to Melody. 'Let's make ourselves pretty,' she said as lightly as she could.

It was an enchanted day, the first of many in the weekends that followed. Lucas seemed to hit just the right note with

Melody, being neither too indulgent or too strict, and Melody took to Greenacres—Lucas's fabulous home with its several acres of grounds—like a duckling to water.

She took huge delight in bossing Lucas's enormous hounds around and fell in love with each one of Martha's cats, as well as Martha herself. And the old woman fully reciprocated the feeling, taking on the role of fussy grandma as though she had been born to it.

Lucas was always the perfect host—relaxed, urbane, amusing and thoughtful, and his kisses—social kisses, Kim assured herself, and not to be confused with anything else—were gentle, warm and totally non-threatening. The kisses of a friend.

After that first Saturday, Kim had tried to refuse further outings but Lucas had simply ignored her protestations with an arrogance that was pure Kane, although she had stuck to her guns about never staying the night at Greenacres. She felt uncomfortable at the thought of waking up in Lucas's home; she felt uncomfortable about a lot of things that were happening. But she kept reassuring herself that Lucas knew exactly where he stood—she couldn't have been more specific.

So all in all it was a magical summer, partly, but with dark surreal undercurrents that sometimes brought Kim wide awake and sweating in the middle of the night.

And then, at the beginning of September, two things happened within a few hours of each other which ripped Kim's fragilely built world apart, and were all the more unexpected for the great weekend she'd just had.

The weekend had started with Maggie phoning her from America on Friday evening to say that Pete had turned up on her doorstep with an engagement ring.

'He can't do without me, Kim.' Maggie had been on such a high the receiver had fairly vibrated. 'Apparently when I left England it prompted him to do some serious thinking and he's been having counselling for his fear of commitment. It brought up all sorts of things, issues he's been burying for years all relating back to his childhood and so on, but he knew he'd lose me if he didn't persevere—so he did!'

'I'm so glad, Maggie.' And she had been.

'He wants us to get married as soon as possible and get a place together. He's so *different*. He's talking about the future, children; I can hardly believe it's Pete.'

'If anyone deserves a happy ending it's you, Maggie,' Kim had said warmly.

'I think he half expected me to contact him in spite of all I said before I left, and when I didn't it convinced him this was make or break time. He'll never know how near I came, time after time, to picking up the phone, though,' Maggie added ruefully. 'He's staying out here with me for a short holiday and then we're flying home together the third week of September, so I'll see you then.'

'What's the ring like?'

'Oh, Kim, it's gorgeous! Three emeralds enclosed by a border of diamonds.'

There was more of the same, and the two women chatted for another two or three minutes before they finished the call. The news gave Kim a warm glow all through the following Saturday, spent at Lucas's home with Melody, and the Sunday when Lucas took them out for Sunday lunch before they visited an antique fair in the afternoon, returning home early because Melody had a headache.

But Monday morning started badly. One of Melody's school shoes disappeared off the face of the earth, a full glass of milk hopped off the breakfast bar and hurled itself on to the floor—according to a tearful Melody—and then Kim couldn't find her car keys. By the time they turned up under a cushion Kim was running half an hour behind schedule, which wouldn't have mattered so much normally but in view of the important meeting due to start promptly at nine in Lucas's office mattered *immensely*.

Since their weekend jaunts, Kim had become almost obsessive about fulfilling all of her responsibilities at the office. The last thing—the very last thing—she wanted was for Lucas to think she was presuming on their relationship; she still hesitated to call it friendship, even in her mind. Friendship should be a pleasantly relaxing, easy, agreeable type of thing, predictable and harmless. Lucas didn't fit one of those criteria.

Kim was constantly on tenterhooks around him, vitally and exhaustingly alive. She was exhilaratingly aware of every little thing about him—the slightest inflexion of his voice which told her the sort of mood he was in, the way his intimidatingly intelligent mind never stopped selecting and storing data, the way he could strike with deadly intent and accuracy. And yet he'd allowed her to see his private side too, that seductive and fascinating part of him that was much more dangerous than anything he displayed in his working life.

On arriving in Kane Electrical's car park, the heavy driving rain exploded into a cloudburst as soon as Kim opened the car door, and in spite of the doors to Reception only being a few yards away her light summer coat was soaked through after her breathless dash.

Great. Raindrops were trickling down her neck and dripping off her fringe as the lift whisked her up to the top floor. Ten minutes past nine and she looked like a drowned rat.

Once in her office she could hear voices from the other room, and after switching on her desk lamp—the morning had turned as dark as night—she hurried into her private cloakroom and stripped off her wet coat, quickly dabbing her fringe and the rest of her hair before peering in the mirror at her damp face.

'Kim?' The knock on the cloakroom door corresponded with Lucas's voice. 'Are you okay?'

Whether it was the irritations and panic of the morning, or the fact that she felt she had been living on a knife-edge ever since she had first come to work for Lucas, or simply that her period was due soon and she was ready to argue with the bricks in the wall, Kim didn't know, but suddenly she felt angry.

She wrenched open the door and glared up into Lucas's face as she said, 'Of course I'm okay. You haven't left them all in there to come and ask me that, have you? What will they think?'

'Think?' He hadn't liked her tone and the chiselled face told her so. 'What on earth are you talking about?'

'I'm talking about you nipping out here,' she snapped back testily, aware she was being horrendously unfair but unable to stop herself. 'They'll either think you're checking up on me or that we're having an affair.'

He stared at her as though she had gone mad. 'In the first place I have never ''nipped'' anywhere in my life,' he said icily, 'and in the second this is the first time you have been later than half past eight in all the time you've worked for me. When I saw a light go on and you still didn't make an appearance, I wondered if you'd had a bump on the way to work in view of the atrocious weather conditions.'

'Well, I haven't.'

'So it appears.' The silver eyes narrowed into slits of light. 'And as for anyone making a judgement on what I do and don't do as far as my secretary is concerned, it's none of their damn business.'

'In other words, you don't care what assumption they might make,' she said frostily, as an errant raindrop trickled down her forehead.

'Don't be ridiculous.' He was really furious now; the grey eyes were positively shimmering with white heat.

'I'm not being ridiculous.' She knew she ought to stop, she knew it but her tongue seemed to have a life of its own. 'You might think it's okay for people to think we're having an affair but I don't! Word has probably already got around that we've been seeing each other out of work; what do you think that looks like to everyone?'

'That we like each other?' Lucas suggested with a silky smoothness that spoke of controlled rage.

'You know what they'll think, especially with your reputation,' she shot back tightly.

'That enough, Kim.' He looked as if he was about to shake her.

'No it's not. Not nearly enough.' She couldn't remember how all this had stared but suddenly she knew this moment had been brewing for weeks, if not months, perhaps from the first days of their relationship when he had started to inveigle himself into her life and into her heart.

She couldn't be what Lucas wanted her to be. She didn't have the will-power or the strength to try, or the courage to face the pain and rejection if he decided she wasn't good enough. Graham had told her she was an empty shell— beautiful packaging with no present inside was how he had described it, once. Useless in bed, frigid, cold—he'd thrown accusation after accusation at her until, in spite of herself, she had begun to believe them. She didn't dare sleep with Lucas and see the disappointment in his eyes...

'Come into my office when you've calmed down and are ready to begin work,' Lucas said with cold emphasis. 'We'll discuss this later.'

'I'm giving you my notice.' Her face was as white as a sheet but her voice was steady. 'And I am calm.'

'You're giving in your notice because I asked you if you were all right?' Lucas bit out incredulously.

'No. Yes. I mean...' She willed herself not to cry, forcing

back the tears with superhuman effort. 'I don't want to work here any more.'

'You don't want to work for *me*,' he said grimly. 'What about Melody?'

'What about her?' she said, sticking her chin out. 'I've paid off the last of the debts—' thanks to his generosity '—and we're solvent again. I can find a job that covers the mortgage and our bills and that's all I want.'

'I meant, what about *me* and Melody?' he rasped tersely. 'It might have escaped your notice but your daughter's got pretty fond of me over the last little while. How is it going to affect her if I disappear out of her life without so much as a by your leave?'

She jerked her head back, her face blazing with a mixture of hot defiance and panic, and it was the panic that made her say the words that cut like a jagged blade. Cruel words, words she didn't mean even as she voiced them. 'So all this has been a ploy to get me into your bed through Melody, has it?' she said in a stony voice that was a cover for the desperate wailing inside. 'You would actually sink so low to use a child to get what you wanted?'

For a moment he stared at her in blank disbelief, and then she saw a rage such as she'd never seen on any human being's face darken his countenance like a terrifying winter storm. He stepped into the small cloakroom, slamming the door behind him as his eyes shot white fire into her frightened face.

'I've taken things from you I've never taken from any woman,' he said with deadly intent, 'and look where it's got me. I thought you needed time, gentleness, like a highly strung thoroughbred that's been abused by a moron in an effort to break its will when what it really needed was careful handling and tender persuasion. I've tried to show you who and what I am—I've bared my soul to you, Kim, and

I've never done that to another woman. What a damn stupid fool I've been.'

'Lucas, please.' She was frightened, terrified. There was such revulsion in his eyes she thought she would die from it.

'And all the time you've had me down as the type of sick individual who manipulates a kid in order to get her mother to service him,' he growled furiously. 'Because that's how you think I view it, isn't it? No finer feelings, no affair of the heart—just bodily needs that require dealing with.'

'I didn't say that,' Kim whispered desperately.

'That's exactly what you said. Well, maybe I'll revert to type, then, eh? Give you the satisfaction of telling yourself you were right all along?'

He pulled her against him without any warning and with such savagery that her head snapped back, exposing the pure line of her neck as her face lifted to his.

The cool restraint that had always been a part of his dealings with her was gone, burnt away by the force of the grenade she had thrown at him, and as she began to struggle in his arms his dark head bent and took her mouth in a fiery kiss.

The memory of that last searing time with Graham was suddenly acutely real, but instead of a wet slimy mouth smothering her face, hard, cruel hands ravaging her body voraciously, this was Lucas. His mouth was dominant and determined but it was lighting a fire that was made up of desire, not fear or revulsion, and his mastery of her body, his strength and virility as he crushed her against him, was sending the fire flickering into every nerve and sinew.

She continued to struggle for a few moments more, confusion and whirling distress at his easy command of her senses, his conquest of her mind and body causing her to try and fight when all real protest was gone, swallowed up in the pleasure that was taking hold.

'You want me, Kim,' he ground out between increasingly intimate kisses. 'You might not like that, you might not like *me*, but you want me nevertheless.'

His hand was cupping her head as he moulded her against him, and she could feel he was already hot and hard and brutally challenging.

'No…' It was feeble, humiliatingly so, and he recognised her weakness, his voice holding a quieter, almost gloating note as he said, 'Yes, oh, yes, my cool little secretary, my elusive ice-queen.'

His hands were ruthlessly exploiting her need of him and she couldn't resist what his hands and mouth were doing to her, arching against him as she finally gave up all efforts to lie to herself and Lucas, her fingers exploring his hard lean body as intimately as his were doing to her.

It was wild and savage and primitive, a delirious longing to get closer and closer to the man she loved and satisfy their mutual need. There was no past and no future, just the close, desperate exploiting of their shared passion, and with every moment that passed, every delicious sensation that was taking her further and further away from anything she had ever known or imagined, she wanted him more.

She was vaguely aware of where she was but somehow it didn't matter, it wasn't real; reality was Lucas's mouth and hands and the things he was doing to her. And then, as she felt him move her back a pace and position her against the wall, she opened her eyes wide. He was going to take her, right now, with a meeting going on next door and anyone liable to come looking for them.

The same thought must have occurred to Lucas.

The hands that were preparing to hoist her skirt upward froze, his breath laboured and ragged as he fought for control. Kim found herself looking straight into his face and the silver-grey eyes were brilliantly clear, their light burning into her brain as she watched him take raw gulps of air.

When he eased himself away from her it was slowly, giving her time to persuade her trembling legs to take her weight without the support of his arms.

He took a step backwards, raking his hair through a couple of times before adjusting the collar of his shirt and then his tie, and all the time Kim watched him with huge disbelieving eyes.

Her body was burning, aching for an assuagement only he could give, and she couldn't believe, she just couldn't take on board that he had stopped.

She saw his hand reach out behind him and open the cloakroom door as he turned, but even when the door began to close again and she was alone she still continued to stand in an attitude of frozen disbelief. And then she began to shake, not so much with the growing feeling of shame that was dawning as the liquid ice of her numbed emotions began to melt and trickle into her bloodstream, but with the knowledge that he was gone, that in the last resort he hadn't wanted her, *he had been able to walk away and leave her.*

CHAPTER TEN

AFTER she had transformed herself into the cool, collected Mrs Allen again Kim walked straight out of the cloakroom and continued out of the building.

It was probably the coward's way out, she told herself, as she drove along the route she had driven just an hour before, but the thought of facing Lucas again was impossible. She would write her formal resignation tonight and for the sake of propriety make the excuse of domestic difficulties making it necessary she leave immediately.

She thought, later, that it was ironic how lies could come back to haunt you.

She took the phone off the hook as soon as she got home, sitting in numb misery for an hour or more before she found the release of tears, and then after a storm of weeping that left her pale-faced and red-eyed she made herself a strong cup of black coffee and took stock.

She had burnt her boats with Lucas. It was consuming, overwhelming and she was frightened at how much it mattered. He had shown her all too succinctly that he could take her or leave her, and he'd decided to leave her. And she couldn't blame him. She really couldn't. When she thought of what she'd said...

She moaned softly, the sound echoing round the sitting room like the cry of a small bewildered hurt animal.

Lucas wasn't like Graham. She stood up quickly, finishing the coffee in a few hard gulps before going upstairs and running a bath. She felt dirty; not because of what she had allowed with Lucas, funnily enough, but because of her accusations. And she hadn't meant them—even as she'd

179

said them she had known she hadn't meant them. But Lucas didn't know that, and he wouldn't believe her now, whatever she said. He must hate her. She moaned again, hot tears coursing down her cheeks.

She continued to cry all the time she lay in the bath, but by the time she was dressed again in jeans and a long loose jumper she had told herself she had to get herself under control.

In the mercurial way of British weather, the fierce storm of the morning had given way to a mild tranquil September day that even promised sunshine for the afternoon, and Kim glanced at her watch as she came downstairs again. Half-past eleven. Six hours to go before she was due to pick up Melody and she would go mad if she spent them brooding in the house.

She glanced at the telephone and as her hand went out to replace the receiver she stopped herself.

She'd write her resignation now and then post it when she went for a walk; Lucas would receive it tomorrow morning. If he was trying to contact her now she didn't want to know; the last thing she could do was to talk to him. She would break down and humiliate herself further, beg him to forgive her or something similar, and he had shown her—in words and action—that he was finished with her.

How come it had taken losing him irrevocably to tell her she was the biggest fool in the world? But then perhaps she had never really had him in the first place? Why would a man like Lucas Kane want her? All the old insecurities and doubts flooded in, but although they tried to convince her she had done the right thing, that finishing this affair that wasn't an affair was the safe and right thing to do, they didn't hold their normal power.

She should have given him—and herself—a chance. The tumult in her breast was sickening as she realised the enormity of her mistake. He had done everything right, everything, and she had thrown it all back in his face.

And Lucas was right. Graham had won. Even from the grave he was still winning. And she had let him, she had aided and abetted him.

Lucas had said he loved her. Whether that would have led to more, to marriage even, she didn't know, but now she never would.

She pulled out her notepaper and envelopes, and before she had time to lose her nerve she wrote Lucas a letter telling him exactly how she felt. She wrenched all the barriers down and bared her soul, exposed herself so completely that she felt she'd become a little child again, vulnerable and unprotected. She didn't beg or plead, she didn't ask to be taken back either in his heart or as his secretary, she just told him how she felt about him. And she finished by saying she was enclosing her letter of resignation. If he wanted to accept it she understood. If he was willing to give her a second chance he could tear it up and let her know accordingly.

Once she had written her notice and sealed the two pieces of paper in the envelope she felt slightly better.

She would go for a walk. It had been ages since she had walked alone in the fresh air, and she would post the envelope while she was out.

She'd made a mess of everything, a terrible, unforgivable mess, and it had separated her—and Melody—from the one man in all the world she would ever love. If Lucas didn't love her enough to forgive her she only had herself to blame; she had given him very little in their one-sided relationship. Her one hope was Lucas himself, because he wasn't like other men. He was head and shoulders above even the best of them.

She left the house quickly, tears trickling down her cheeks again, but once she was walking in the mild

September afternoon the tears dried up, although the sick churning in her stomach didn't get any better.

After posting the letter she went for a walk on nearby woodland that housed an adventure playground, sitting for some time on one of the wooden benches overlooking the children's playing area with the weak sun warming her face and the musky smell of wet vegetation wafting on the autumn breeze.

It was nearly four o'clock when she ventured home, and as she turned the corner of the street and saw a car parked outside her house she only gave it a cursory glance. The red Cavalier was not a car she recognised.

It was only as she turned on to her drive that the car door opened and Charlie, Lucas's caretaker at the plant, called her name.

'Charlie?' Kim stared at him in absolute amazement. 'What on earth are you doing here?' she asked, walking over to the car and peering in at his hoary face. 'How did you know where I live?'

'The boss told me.' It was the way Charlie always referred to Lucas. 'He was looking for you earlier. He's been ringing you all day, from what I can make out, and after he'd come here and you weren't in, I said I'd come and wait outside.'

'You did?' Kim was completely lost but there was something in the old man's face that was alarming her. 'I don't understand.'

'He'd have come back himself but he thought he'd be more use at the hospital,' Charlie said disjointedly. 'And he didn't want everyone sticking their oar in, nosy lot some of 'em, but you know how he talks to me. Go back a long way, me and the boss. Known him since he was a nipper.' And then, as though that had reminded him, he said quietly, 'It's your little 'un, love. Don't get yourself in a panic, but she was a bit poorly at school.'

'Melody?' Kim's face drained of colour. 'Where is she?'

'At the hospital—that's where I'm to take you, the boss says.'

'Oh, Charlie.' Kim found she was gripping the top of the car door like a lifeline.

Charlie drove to the hospital as though he was competing in Formula One, and once there Kim was whisked away by a sympathetic-faced nurse and led through a bewildering maze of corridors to the children's wards. The nurse would say nothing beyond Melody had been taken ill at school and they were doing some tests, but the sister who met her at the entrance to the unit was more forthcoming.

'Suspected meningitis,' she said very softly after she'd told Kim Melody was in an isolation room. 'Another child from Melody's class was brought in with the same thing during the night and the school was informed first thing, fortunately. Has Melody been poorly at all over the last day or two? A little off-colour or feverish?'

'She's been a little tired, headachey,' Kim said numbly, feeling like the worst mother in the world. 'I wanted to keep her off school this morning, actually, but there were tears and she insisted she wanted to go. They were choosing children for the country dancing display at the summer fête next week.'

The sister nodded understandingly. She'd had children herself. 'It was only at midday she was taken really poorly,' she said quietly, 'but with the school having been informed about the other child they decided not to take any chances, so when they couldn't contact you she was admitted. Wise decision, in the event, but she's now on antibiotics and she'll be fine so try not to worry. This is easy to treat if it's caught early enough, but in some cases it worsens very rapidly, especially in babies and children as young as Melody.'

'Can....can I see her?' Kim asked faintly.

'Of course. Your fiancé has been with her almost from
when she was brought in, so she hasn't been alone for the
tests, Mrs Allen. I think it would have been easier to prise
a bear cub away from its mother than Melody from Mr
Kane,' she added a trifle drily.

Her fiancé? Kim gazed at the small brisk woman bewilderedly but said nothing.

When Kim entered the small, white sterile room, Lucas
rose immediately from the chair at the side of the bed, but
not before Kim saw he had been holding one small dimpled
hand between his own.

Melody was fast asleep, her fair hair spread out over the
regulation hospital pillow and her thick eyelashes resting
on flushed cheeks. She didn't actually look ill at all, Kim
thought faintly, as she walked over and stood looking down
at the small figure, tears streaming down her pale cheeks.

'It's okay; they've told you it's okay?' Lucas said softly
as he came and stood beside her, his arm round her shoulders.

'Oh, Lucas.' She turned into his arms, sobbing uncontrollably, and he held her very tightly until she calmed
down, by which time the sister had left and they were alone.
He put her from him a little, looking down at her with intent
compelling eyes as he said, 'She's *really* going to be all
right, Kim. It's not a sop, okay? I've checked with everyone
in authority and they've caught it in the early stages, due
to the warning of the other child.'

There was another silence but still she couldn't speak,
the tears sparkling on her cheeks like tiny diamonds. 'I'm
sorry.' It was a faint whisper but he still heard it.

'This is not your fault, Kim. You weren't to know.'

'I mean...I mean about us, this morning, everything. I...I
can't believe I said all that.'

'You're sorry? When I practically raped you,' he said
with a rough softness that spoke of inner torment. 'When

I sent you racing off to goodness knows where? I'll never forgive myself—'

'It wasn't like that.' She felt paralysed by all the emotion of the day, utterly spent, but she couldn't let him take any blame for something that had been all her fault. 'It was me. I was horrible,' she said brokenly. 'I said horrible things.'

'Because I made you,' he said gruffly, his voice shaking. 'You never lied to me, Kim. You were totally honest from day one, making it quite clear you didn't want to get involved with any man. But in my arrogance I thought because I loved you so much I could make you love me. I couldn't believe I could feel the way I did and it wouldn't affect you. I used the physical attraction between us to try and make you look at me as a man rather than just your employer.'

'I...I do.'

'As a friend, I know.' He took a deep hard breath and then they both stilled as the tiny figure in the bed sighed softly, before falling back into a deeper sleep.

'Not as a friend,' said Kim in a shaky whisper. He had said he loved her. Did he still love her? 'I...I love you, Lucas. I have done almost from when we met but I was too scared and hung up on everything that's happened in the past to believe it could work. Graham...some of the things he said and did—I couldn't believe any man would want me if they knew what I was really like. He said I was frigid, a pretty parcel with nothing inside.'

He was looking at her with incredulity stamped all over his hard, handsome face, and that, more than the words that followed, convinced Kim how wrong, how terribly misguided, she had been to ever link Graham and Lucas in her mind for one moment.

Lucas was the sort of man who loved for ever. She had trampled his male pride into the ground this morning and made him hate himself in the process, and yet—believing it was all over between them and that she loathed him—he had come to Melody's side to be with her because he knew Kim couldn't. He could be a hard man, and ruthless, but with her and with Melody he had been wonderful.

'Kim, I love you more than I can ever say and I always will,' Lucas said with quiet emphasis. 'I want to marry you and have children with you and grow old with you. I want to know you are my wife and I have the right to cherish and protect you and take care of you and our family. I love you more than life, Kim. It kills me that you've had to go through what you have, but I'll spend the rest of my life making it up to you, if you'll let me.'

'I…I thought you wouldn't want me any more, after this morning. You stopped—' She couldn't go on but she didn't have to.

'I stopped because I suddenly realised what I was doing,' he said softly, his voice husky and the faint accent that occasionally flavoured his words giving a smoky undertone to what he was saying. 'I didn't want our first time to be like that, Kim, even if it was going to be our only time,' he added with faint ruefulness. 'I'd lost control. I was angry; it made me no better than Graham—'

'No, don't say that, not ever.' She placed a finger on his lips, her voice breaking. 'You're the best there is, Lucas.'

His mouth sought hers and he kissed her with gentle reassurance at first, holding her close as he whispered his love against her lips, and then more passionately as she melted against him. 'Earth and heaven might disappear, my love, the moon might stop shining and the sun might fall into the ocean, but I'll never stop loving you,' he murmured after a time as they drew away to look into each other's faces.

They talked and kissed some more before Lucas brought another chair close to the bed, so they could sit together. 'I feel like she's my child, too,' Lucas whispered softly, turning away from the little figure in the bed as he lifted Kim's chin and met her eyes. 'Right from the first time I saw her, and I could swear she feels the same. I nearly went crazy when I first got here before they said everything was going to be okay.'

'You said you were my fiancé?' Kim murmured quietly.

'I hadn't got time to worry about red tape or any rules about only family. Melody needed one of us,' Lucas said with Kane disregard for convention.

'Oh, Lucas.'

'I'd like to adopt her legally, Kim, so she takes my name after we're married.'

'Oh, *Lucas*.' Kim smiled tremulously.

It was much, much later when Melody awoke properly, but Kim and Lucas were still sitting by the bed, Lucas's arm holding Kim tight and her blonde head resting against his shoulder as she slept. His other hand was clasped tight in Kim's.

Melody surveyed them sleepily and Lucas smiled at her, saying, 'Hi, sweetheart. You feeling better now?'

'Uh-huh.' Melody nodded drowsily, her brown eyes going again to their clasped hands and her mother's sleeping face. Kerry's mummy and daddy held hands. 'Lucas?'

'Yes, sweetheart?'

'Are you going to be my new daddy?'

'You bet your sweet life I am, sweetheart.'

'*Scrumptious!*'

$ Saving Money $
Has Never Been
This Easy!

Just fill out and send in this form from any October, November and December 2002 books and we will send you a coupon booklet worth a total savings of $20.00 off future purchases of Harlequin and Silhouette books in 2003.

Yes! It's that easy!

I accept your incredible offer!
Please send me a coupon booklet:

Name (PLEASE PRINT)

Address   Apt. #

City   State/Prov.   Zip/Postal Code

**In a typical month, how many
Harlequin and Silhouette novels do you read?**

❏ **0-2**   ❏ **3+**

097KJKDNC7   097KJKDNDP

Please send this form to:
   In the U.S.: Harlequin Books, P.O. Box 9071, Buffalo, NY 14269-9071
   In Canada: Harlequin Books, P.O. Box 609, Fort Erie, Ontario L2A 5X3

Allow 4-6 weeks for delivery. Limit one coupon booklet per household. Must be postmarked no later than January 15, 2003.

HARLEQUIN®
Makes any time special®

Silhouette®
Where love comes alive™

© 2002 Harlequin Enterprises Limited

PHQ402

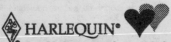